ALL YOUR FRIENDS ARE HERE

stories by M.Shaw

Cover & Interior Art by Echo Echo
Edited by Alex Woodroe

Content warnings are available at the end of this book. Please consult this list for any particular subject matter you may be sensitive to.

TENEBROUS

PRESS

All Your Friends Are Here © 2024 by M.Shaw and Tenebrous Press.

All rights reserved. No parts of this publication may be reproduced, distributed or transmitted in any form by any means, except for brief excerpts for the purpose of review, without the prior written consent of the owner. All inquiries should be addressed to tenebrouspress@gmail.com.

Published by Tenebrous Press.
Visit our website at www.tenebrouspress.com.

Production of this novel was made possible in part by a grant from the Regional Arts & Culture Council. Visit https://racc.org/ for more information.

First Printing, December 2024.

The characters and events portrayed in this work are fictitious. Any similarity to real persons, living or dead, is coincidental and not intended by the author.

Print ISBN: 978-1-959790-19-8
eBook ISBN: 978-1-959790-20-4

Cover art and interior illustrations by Echo Echo.

Edited by Alex Woodroe.

Formatting by Lori Michelle.

All creators in this publication have signed an AI-free agreement. To the best of our knowledge, this publication is free from machine-generated content.

TABLE OF CONTENTS

Introduction by the Author 1
Roots in the Ground 5
The Motorist 16
Man vs. Bomb 38
One Long Staircase, Just Going Up 44
The Only Friend You Ever Need 50
Go With the Flow 72
As I Wait For the Killing Blow 84
My Dad Bought a Space Shuttle 89
The Cure for Loneliness 97
Ready Player (n+1) 114
The Apology 140
Apartémon 151
Objects at Rest 159
Acknowledgements 179
About the Creators 181
Acknowledgement of Original Publication 182
Content Warnings 183

For Lyle

INTRODUCTION

M.Shaw

I'VE SPENT MOST of my life looking for friends and getting myself in trouble in the process. As a teen, it became clear very quickly that I was never going to be cool, and that I could expect a lot of bullying. But it also became clear that I could make people laugh, especially when I was being edgy and morbid, so I leaned into that. It wasn't exactly a way to develop close personal bonds with anyone, but it helped stave off ostracism and loneliness during a phase of life when those things are in generous supply. Adolescence sucks, and going through it in Ohio double-sucks, but I could at least find little oases of peace in my ability to mock society and grin back at death.

Then Eric Harris and Dylan Klebold shot up Columbine High School, and suddenly I was public enemy number one. Not because anyone thought I was going to go on a killing spree, mind you, but because school administrators wanted to assure anxious parents that they were Taking This Seriously and Doing Something, and there I was with my black clothes and violent comic books and troubled disciplinary history. The water of my oasis had been poisoned by moral panic, and I was going to be trapped in it for about the next decade, which is its own entire book and not something I can neatly fit into an introduction.

It's really no wonder that I'm drawn to the absurd, especially given the fact that, 25 years later, the society I inhabit only ever seems to get worse. The stories in this book were written from within my own bafflement about that very fact.

The oldest story in here, "The Only Friend You Ever Need," was

M. SHAW

first published by Crossed Genres Magazine in 2011, back when I was enmeshed in a deeply codependent relationship and still very much devoted to finding a place for myself in a city that, for somewhat related reasons, I will probably never set foot in again. The story itself holds a special place for me, because I wrote it from inside the belly of the metaphorical beast, looking at the life that was offered to me and asking if it was really worth the comfort of personal security when the price was giving up everything that makes life worth actually living. I wasn't going to stop asking that question any time soon, as I imagine will become clear to you very shortly.

Some of these stories were first written at Clarion, the writing workshop at UC San Diego where my cup overflowed with joyful community on a daily basis while the world continued to go to shit in the background, both in terms of my personal life and the various socio-political realities I share with the rest of us. Stories like "The Motorist" and "Apartémon" came out of the quiet feeling of uneasiness that underscored that time in my life, the constant suspicion that there is a set of jaws closing around you even in the midst of new connections.

Others, like "The Cure for Loneliness," emerged during the onset of the COVID-19 pandemic. Though it was (and is!) a time of impossible trauma, as the disease killed and disabled people en masse, there was also, for me, an odd sense of relief to the days before the world decided to stop paying attention. So many people had to grapple with the isolation and paranoia that had been a feature of my daily life for so long, that it felt, in a very uncomfortable way, that others were finally beginning to see the world as I saw it.

I don't think it's a coincidence that that particular story is, as of right now, the only one I've written that has been published in a language other than English (Japanese, in this case, thanks to Hayakawa Publishing and translator Hisashi Kujirai's superb work). It's also the only one for which I have framed fan art hanging on my wall at home. It's a very odd variety of gratification, to have these reminders of how many people have read the story and said to themselves, "Now here is someone who understands what it's like to quietly go insane in a one-bedroom apartment with only plants, taxidermy, and self-absorbed exes for company."

INTRODUCTION

Much like the downtrodden commuters in "The Apology," or the unhinged restaurant staff and patrons in "Objects at Rest," there is something to the feeling that we are, for better or worse, all in this together that helps the worst of times become bearable—even when it's maybe not a good thing to simply bear it instead of letting the pain and sorrow rage out of control, as they eventually must.

My children are stories, not people, which is why I'm not burdened with the expectation of loving them all equally. That's why it's easy for me to admit that what I'm most excited for, here, is *Ready Player (n+1)*, a novelette original to this collection. That's where all the sensibilities you'll see on display in this book finally coalesced into a single 10,000-word primal scream of a narrative about the false promises of safety and nostalgia, the cultural blunt force of capitalism, and the need to sing over the bones (to borrow a motif from folklore). This is the one where it all goes balls-out (or neovagina-out, in this particular case) and my dearest hope is that you'll get the urge to share its lack of giving a fuck with rooms full of people while getting playfully electrocuted, as I once did.

In case it was at all unclear, this is not a book for normal people. I think that's a good thing. If you're reading this, then on some level it's because darkness and absurdity feel familiar to you, especially when you catch them peeking out from behind the many masks we're compelled to cover them with in today's world.

Welcome to the kingdom of the broken. I've been here a while, and I'm happy to show you around. Check out our commercial space shuttle launch site, our McMansions under permanent construction, our nudist dendrophile cult, the valley where we keep our killer grandmas, our full-contact spectator zombie races, and the giant picnic basket where The 500 Richest Earth Men host their fiscal orgies. It's not an easy place to be, but it's a hell of a lot better than a starring role in the rat race at the end of history, and all your friends are here.

ROOTS IN THE GROUND

THE SUN MUST have been down about an hour, but we were nowhere near giving up. We held the line, swept the mountain sector by sector, sucking in breath after breath of frigid, pine-scented air and expelling it, warm, bearing the missing hiker's name.

We all had work the next day, but October was still shoulder season, so at least there wouldn't be tourists pounding on the door of every business in town first thing. The hiker was an out-of-towner. None of us were clued into what their business was here. They hadn't brought skis or a mountain bike, neither of which would be of much use that time of year anyway. They'd come alone. If Carla Jeffries, who owned the B&B, hadn't been such a busybody, then we might never have known they were gone.

The group I was with swept uphill along the south ridge. The ridge flattened out halfway to the peak, but the trees only got thicker from there to the treeline. It was in that dense part of the woods that someone's flashlight beam caught a human shape. Janice blew the whistle to call a halt, and we all ran toward the sound. When I reached the spot, we were looking at the backside of a fully naked man, pressed against the trunk of a cottonwood tree. At first, we assumed it was the hiker, but then our lights found another person in a similarly compromised position. Then another, and another, and another. There were fourteen, at my count, and not a scrap of clothing on a single one.

Janice got on the radio, while the rest of us stood speechless and staring, and told the other teams that the whistle had been a false alarm. Probably for the best. Some of them included high school kids.

One by one, the naked men and women noticed our presence

and turned to face us. Their fronts were covered with dirt, and quite a few freely bleeding cuts and scrapes.

"Who's got the first aid kit?" I called out. No one responded, but, to be fair, no one had probably expected me to volunteer for the search party. I hadn't exactly been high-functioning for the past twenty years, ever since my wife died and our little Hannah, five at the time, started spending more time with her imaginary friend than her drunk, depressed dad who talked about her dead mom nonstop. Talked *to* her dead mom, on the worst days. But this was the year I'd finally convinced Hannah to come back from the west coast for a Thanksgiving visit, and I guess that lit a fire in me when it came to finding lost people. Still, it was my fourth or fifth recovery attempt, so I couldn't blame anyone for being a little wary.

One of the naked men approached us. The other . . . nudists, I guess, kept their eyes so focused on him that it almost looked like they didn't see us at all. The man wasn't familiar, certainly not from town. "What are you doing here?" he asked.

Personally, I wasn't sure it was even advisable to talk to these people, much less answer their questions. Being part of a search party was an unusual enough situation; throw in whatever this was, and a guy could be forgiven for not knowing what to do.

"We're looking for a lost hiker," said Janice.

"I see," said the naked man. "Well, none of us is a lost hiker."

"And what are *you* doing out here?" said Janice.

"Do you maybe want to put some clothes on?" Dave Cleary added.

The naked man ignored Dave. "If it's any of your business, we *were* in the middle of an orgy."

"Jeez Louise," said Dave. Most of us were saying something to that effect, but Dave was standing closest to me.

"An orgy," said Janice.

"Roots in the ground," said the naked man, as if this clarified anything.

I swept my flashlight beam between the bodies present. Most were middle age, and looked exactly like the kind of people you'd expect to populate a town like ours, though none of them did. "I don't recognize any of you," I said.

"That doesn't surprise me," said the naked man who, at least, was willing to acknowledge that I had said anything. "Look, your

ROOTS IN THE GROUND

hiker isn't here, so . . . " He shrugged, hands held palm-up, an almost cartoonish gesture. "Would you mind?"

"Just a moment," said Janice, signaling for us clothed people to huddle up together.

Anne Borden spoke first. "He did say they were having an orgy, right?"

"It's below freezing out here," said Dave.

"Their nipples've gotta be hard enough to cut glass," said Ted Furrier.

"Thank you, Ted," said Janice, "thank you for that contribution. Anybody here replacing a windowpane tonight?" She didn't wait for an answer. "How do y'all suggest we handle this? I don't know what the hell's going on, but if we leave them here, they'll be a dozen popsicles covered in infected gashes by morning."

"Something's not right about this," said Ted. "That's all I'm saying."

A few of us cleared our throats. There was a whole host of not-right-here things about this, but what could we do? Even if they wanted our help, there were only three survival blankets in the first aid kit.

"Fuck it," said Dave, "why don't we leave 'em? Freezing or not, I don't want nothin' to do with whatever this is. I mean, not that I'm well acquainted with these things, but doesn't an orgy normally involve . . . you know . . . " He made an O with his thumb and forefinger, then poked his other forefinger through the hole.

"Fucking!" said Ted. "Exactly! What kind of orgy is this? They're just rubbing themselves on the trees, looks like."

"The way they're all scratched up," said Dave. "They trying to diddle the trees?"

I pointed my flashlight back toward the nudists, guessing maybe I could do some forensic shit on their wounds—I'm not a CSI, I just watch too much TV. "Hold up," I said, "look."

Our lights lit the trees. Fourteen naked bodies had been reduced to just a few stragglers, weaving between the trees away from us, up the slope.

"I guess that's that," said Dave.

Ted must not have been listening, because he took off after the fleeing nudists, followed by Anne and a few others.

"Do *not*—" said Janice. "Hey! *Hey!* Fuckin' hell."

"Good riddance, I say," said Dave. "I mean the weirdos, not our folks."

"Should we follow?" I asked.

"Absolutely not," said Janice. "We stick with the plan, keep sweeping our grid. They're in front of us, so eventually either we'll run into them, or another team will. Provided no one else wants to do anything astonishingly stupid."

We re-formed the line, spaced appropriately farther apart to account for the deserters. We kept calling for the missing hiker, but it's safe to say that was no longer the first thing on my mind. I kept thinking about the way they'd all stood there, stark naked and bleeding in the cold, like they weren't the least bit uncomfortable. As we poked through the woods, I kept looking for any discarded garments left behind, but never saw a single one. Had they somehow grabbed all their clothes as they ran, or had they never had them? Either way, where the hell had they come from, and where the hell were they going?

All I knew for sure was how I felt, which was that I wanted to get myself off that mountain and not look back. I told myself it was just my old chickenshit depression trying to give me an excuse to cloister myself at home and avoid the world, and that I should push on like an adult instead. Despite what the horror movies of the 1970s would have us believe, a bunch of naked hippies in the woods probably aren't planning a Satanic murder party, no matter how scary they look.

I tried to go back to thinking about Hannah, how I'd tell this story to her in a few weeks. Oddly enough, I found this making me feel more uneasy, not less.

I'd lost track of how much time had passed when Dave tripped on a root and busted his nose. Janice called a halt so we could check him out, stick some gauze in his nostrils and bandage his ankle.

"How you feeling?" I asked him, pressing the ends of a strip of surgical tape to his cheekbones.

"Little dizzy," he said. Dave was in pretty good shape for his age, but still forging well into his sixties. Thankfully he didn't object when Janice drew the line and said they wouldn't continue the search until he headed back to town.

"You know the way?" she said.

ROOTS IN THE GROUND

Dave mumbled something that might have been *yeah*, but was really more like "nyeh," which just as easily could have been *nah*.

"I'll make sure he gets there okay," I said.

"Oh come on," said Dave, shooting me a knitted-brows look that strongly implied, *Seriously? You of all people are going to look after me?* "You stick with the group, I'll do fine on my own."

"Yeah, I know all about doing fine on your own," I said. Dave shrugged, which was as good as I was going to do.

I didn't make the connection at the time, but when Hannah was little she had this song about trees. As far as anyone could tell, she'd made it up. It was cute. Kind of like a love song to a tree, as if it were a close friend or maybe a boyfriend. The kind of thing kids come up with, when they're still figuring out how to process feelings like affection and attachment.

The title of the song was "Roots in the Ground." The lyrics changed over time along with the artist, but the chorus was always that phrase, repeated 8 times at increasing volume. The last "roots in the ground!" was a scream. It was *cute*.

Janice swore the group would be fine without us, even considering they were down by almost half between this and the ones running after the nudists. She pointed out they'd be getting those folks back, hopefully before too long.

I didn't say so to anyone, but I was glad for the excuse to hike back down with Dave. Something the naked man said had plucked a chord in me that hadn't been plucked in a long time, and not a pleasant one. I was ready to give in to my chickenshit depression, by that point. I had thoughts milling around in my head that I didn't want to be there, and the sooner I could get home, eat a gummy and watch some stupid TV show, the better.

Dave found a walking stick before long and insisted it was all the support he needed. We hiked on in silence. I made sure to keep myself busy, sweeping my flashlight in all directions, still looking for our hiker because it was better than thinking about something else, like why those people had looked so familiar even though I couldn't identify a single one of them.

We were still the better part of an hour from the base area, probably more considering that one of us was in hobbling shape. The cold wasn't doing us any favors, either. At least we were well outside of rattlesnake season.

That being the case, one could imagine my surprise when I heard something off in the trees that sounded very much like a rattlesnake. Dave stopped in his tracks the same moment I did, so he must have heard it too. A moment later it came again, that crisp, cascading shudder. Unmistakable.

"You gotta be kidding me," said Dave. "What now?"

It took a minute for me to get my light on it, far back in the trees as it was. Faint movement. Not a snake; even from a distance I could tell I was looking at skin, not scales.

"I think it's a person," I said.

"Jimminy Christmas," said Dave.

I kept my light trained on the source of the sound and started toward it, cautioning Dave to watch his step.

It was one of the nudists from before. Or so I assumed, given her lack of clothing and prominence of wounds. How she had doubled back and passed us without our noticing was beyond me, but it was either that or there were multiple tree orgies going on that night, which I didn't want to entertain. She looked in even worse shape than before. There were trails of blood running out of her ears and nostrils. The rattling noise came from her heaving breath, passing through all the blood in her mouth, which visibly bubbled and sputtered on each exhale. Trembling hands held a stick that she was working back and forth over her privates. Most of her fingernails were torn off. Her skin had gone bright red from the cold, with the exception of her feet, which were blue, fading into black.

"I'm out," said Dave.

"Hold up," I said, but when I turned, all I found was his back as he fumbled his way out of the trees.

"Too old for this shit!" he called back.

So he said, but the woman on the ground couldn't have been any younger than him. A large and vocal part of my brain wanted me to leave her for dead right then, which I ignored. Unsettling

ROOTS IN THE GROUND

though it was to stay there, I knew that any future reports of her death from exposure would be on my conscience. She still wasn't doing anything besides rubbing herself with the stick and making that godawful rattle. It had an audible wheeze underneath, I was noticing.

Dave might have been out of earshot, but I tried. "You better make it back to town, asshole! You get lost, that's on you!"

No response. Just the sound of breath, pushed through a mouthful of blood.

I didn't have any supplies on me beyond the flashlight and my phone. I could call 911, but who could they send? All the first responders in town were already on the mountain, and Dave had taken our radio. There was no way the woman would be able to walk on those feet, given that they were starting to resemble overripe eggplants in shape and color.

I knelt by her and shone my light in her face. Confirmed: I had absolutely no idea who she was. Like her compatriots, though, looking at her gave me the oddest feeling that she *should* be familiar. Her pupils, which had been dilated across the entire iris, shrank to pinpricks when the light hit them. No reaction otherwise.

"Hey," I said, "can you hear me? Can you sit up?"

She coughed. Blood from her mouth spattered across my face.

"Jesus!" I shot to my feet, wiping desperately at the blood with the sleeve of my Carhartt.

Something came out of her throat, which sounded like either pained retching or the word *almost* or both. Then, more clearly, "Please. Please, it must be enough."

I stood over her again, making sure to keep my face a good distance from hers. Blood had splashed onto her chin and chest as well, enough that it was already forming rivulets. I took a step toward her and my foot sank into the ground, almost to the ankle, before I yanked it back. All around her, the dirt felt soft, damp. I smelled something rotten, which could have been the blood drying on my face but reminded me more of dead leaves.

The best solution I could see here was to put my coat on her and carry her piggyback into town as fast as I could. Getting her onto my back would be complicated, and there was the concern about her coughing blood on me again, but what the hell. I slid a hand under her shoulder and started to lift.

"No!" she screamed.

I stumbled and fell backward.

Her eyeballs wrenched sideways in my direction, though when I shone my light on her face they looked cloudy, staring into the distance. My ass stayed firmly planted on a pile of pine needles.

"Got separated." Her voice was a deep, witchy croak. She burned through words like they were holding her up. "When we ran. Lost the sheltering. But I'm so close."

My hands groped behind me, searching for anything that might impede my scooting backward while I kept eyes on her. I realized, as I was doing this, that I had ceased to feel much of anything other than fear. My whole body was swimming with adrenaline, and it felt so terrifyingly peaceful. I wasn't even cold anymore.

"Please," she said again, followed by something that was either gagging, or a word made up entirely of vowels. "I accept your embrace. Please."

Her entire face contracted, except for her mouth, which shot open. Her back arched. Either she was having a seizure, or that knobby old stick was really doing something for her. Blood pushed itself from every open wound, dark and halfway clotted.

If that was all I'd seen, it would have been enough. I could have stood at that moment and booked it into town and left her to the frozen woods. I've still got enough cowardice in me for that. But I didn't, God help me.

Here's the thing: kids say creepy shit all the time, especially when they're little. All the more so when there's a dead parent involved. It's normal. It's healthy, or so the shrink said. Hannah's imaginary friend showed up about as soon as she was old enough to talk, but their relationship shifted into a new gear when her mom died. This made perfect sense to me. It also made sense that the imaginary friend in question was a bit morbid.

"Rudy," as she called it (*it*, not *him*), was made of nothing. She would get really mad if you tried to ask what Rudy looked like. One time she cried because her first grade teacher said "Rudy doesn't look like anything," which Hannah insisted was not at all the same as looking like nothing. If you said anything about Rudy that she

ROOTS IN THE GROUND

didn't like, she'd stomp out of the room and scream that she was going to The Sheltering, which I assumed was where Rudy lived, probably a word she'd heard on some cartoon.

If you asked her what Rudy did with its time, you'd learn that it ate sticks, dead leaves, and animal bones. Its favorite activity was "gardening," but if you asked for clarification then it turned out this involved burying things—seeds, toys, dead animals or anything else—and growing them back as trees. Rudy's penis was also a tree, which got Hannah into trouble at school on multiple occasions. The funnest aspect of the penis thing was that it wasn't connected to Rudy's body, and it didn't stay in one location; it could be any tree, anywhere on the mountain. Rudy didn't like us for living on the mountain, but it didn't want us to leave, either.

You can see where we assumed that this was all about her mom's death. The fixation with burial, with things that were dead and rotting, the central importance of someone being "nothing" and yet all around you at once. Almost *too* easy to analyze, and I wasn't even the shrink.

Like all imaginary friends, Rudy went away after a while. She might have hung onto it a bit longer than most kids, but again, that was understandable. Her friendship with Rudy could even be cute at times, although no one was exactly sorry to see it go.

After that night on the mountain, I wasn't so sure it had.

The woman fell limp, letting out a sigh like wind in a blizzard. Then something settled on top of her.

It was more like the lack of a something, really. All the light was sucked out of the space just above her body. It was the kind of darkness so thick that it seemed to have its own substance, beyond mere absence of light. At the same time, looking at it hurt my eyes like looking at a bare lightbulb. Like looking at the Sun. When I pointed my flashlight at her, it showed nothing. The thing on top of her refused to be illuminated, beyond a slight shimmer at its edges where the light was devoured.

There was a heavy creaking sound, and the ground beneath her receded, as if it were simply falling away into nothing. She sunk into the dirt, and with the darkness on top of her, it looked almost like she dissolved. Then everything was quiet.

When I stood, my vision had gone fuzzy. I didn't feel weak or tired, but my strength was gone. Moving felt more like operating a puppet. My vision warped and crackled around the periphery. I looked into the hole in the ground where the woman had been. A few inches below the edge was a thick latticework of roots. Couldn't see much past that. I thought, *Huh*. Then I turned and started walking. Next thing I remember, I was back home.

I slept on it. Multiple nights, in fact. Let it never be said that cutting my daughter out of my life forever was something I did on impulse. After what happened in the ensuing days, I had to harden my heart. I had to keep her away from the mountain.

They never found the missing hiker. By the next morning, most folks didn't remember there ever was a missing hiker, and the ones who did talked about the search in distant terms, like something that happened years ago. They never found any of the nudists, either. As far as I can tell, I'm the only one who remembers them at all. I've learned not to bring it up. Dave Cleary never made it back to town, nor did any of the folks who chased after the nudists. No one reported them missing. To this day, all you'll get in return for asking about them will be comments about the weather.

Nothing prepares you for hearing your daughter's voice knowing it's the last time. I've heard you can tell by someone's voice on the phone when they're smiling, even though you can't see them. I don't know if that's true, but Hannah's voice did sound different to me on that call, and I like to remember her smiling.

"Hey dad, what's up?"

"Hi, Hannah! Just wanted to check in, see if you're still thinking of coming home for Thanksgiving?"

A chuckle, with just a hint of annoyance. "Well like I said, *home* is Oakland. I'm coming *to visit* for Thanksgiving."

"That's real good, sweetie. Just making sure. You know we've missed you, all these years."

"We?"

ROOTS IN THE GROUND

"Your mother and I are really looking forward to having you back."

Silence on the line.

"Dad, what the fuck?"

"I know it hasn't been *too* too long, but we still talk about you every night at dinner."

"Dad, quit. You promised, you . . . you wouldn't . . . "

"Sorry, what did we promise? Maybe you told mom, but I can't remember."

Her voice changed again, and this time she definitely wasn't smiling. "I already bought the fucking plane ticket."

"Great! We'll meet you at security."

"I . . . " A long, wet sniff. "I can't do this."

Click.

I can't picture Dave Cleary's face anymore. I can barely remember what Hannah's mom looked like, and her name is gone. Everyone gone is fading, like an imaginary friend. But not Hannah. I remember every day I spent with her, even if most of them weren't great. The pain of it bites deep as ever. That's how I know she's safe.

I don't leave the house much anymore. Most folks assume I'm lapsing back into my old ways, probably over Hannah canceling her visit. They don't know it's because I can feel the trees watching me out there, both of us waiting patiently for the mountain, and whatever's under it, to wrap me in pine and take me in.

THE MOTORIST

SOMETIMES SHAME WILL surprise you. I had imagined this exact situation before, repeatedly if not regularly: sirens in the parking lot, red and blue lights strobing in my bedroom window, me watching myself beat off in the mirror, wearing the lavender seashell lingerie set. In my imagination, I was secure and confident. I stood, put on my sweats and a t-shirt, walked downstairs, opened the door, and talked to the cops about whatever was going on. Just like that, with my lingerie on under my clothes. Maybe my shirt was white and they could see my bra through it. Maybe they could see the bulge of my still-hard dick. I didn't care. Actually, I wanted them to see. My imaginary self knew who I was and what I wanted. Life had taken a lot from me, but it wasn't going to take autoerotic crossdressing, and I didn't care who knew it.

Real me acted more like a teenager caught with porn. Here I was, presented with the very scenario from my weird fantasies, right down to my choice of garments for the evening, and it turned out I wasn't secure or confident at all. I panicked. I stuffed my dick back inside my panties, which was silly because the next instant I kicked the panties off, practically flung the bra over my head (I heard a rip), popped the cover off the intake vent by the bed and stashed the whole getup inside. I got my long johns out of the closet and put them on instead, then put the sweats over that.

I walked downstairs, sweating in the summer heat, heart pounding.

They weren't there for me, of course. They were there for my neighbor, Bob. And why *would* they have come for me, I asked myself as I stood on the porch, watching four officers surround Bob's Honda Fit, each with a flashlight in one hand while the other

THE MOTORIST

rested casually at their hip, next to their holstered gun. I wasn't doing anything wrong. I'd *worked* on this. Not only was it perfectly legal, it was none of their business anyway.

"Finally," said Brent, my other neighbor. He was standing on his porch, in the row of townhouses across the narrow, grassy courtyard from mine, arms folded over his bare chest. He turned to face me, his small, hairy belly swinging in the cool night air. "Can you believe the smell coming off that car?"

"Smell?" Now that Brent mentioned it, there was a stale, fleshy odor hanging around the complex. I realized I had smelled it before, and decided it must be coming from the dog food factory up north of town.

One officer knocked on the car's window. Why, I asked myself as my heartbeat returned to normal, were they so interested in a parked car in the complex lot?

I saw the window roll down.

"Always in that damn car," Brent mumbled. "They way it smells, I swear he must be pissing and shitting in there. Or worse. I mean, I'm not saying he's got a dead body in the trunk, but come on."

As the officer at the window spoke to Bob, another cop walked over to me. I tried to stop myself from panicking. Was I some kind of secondary objective for them? To take me down while they were here? The officer approaching me was a woman, which terrified me, because what if she had found out about my hobbies? Was she offended?

"Good evening, sir," she said, with what might have been a note of accusation.

"Uh, hi. Hello," I said. "I'm Bruce."

"You the one who called?"

"It was me!" said Brent. He stomped across the grass to my porch, which might have looked more authoritative if he were wearing something besides pajama bottoms and slippers. "I called. Thank you for your service, officer."

What a suck-up, I thought. What did he have against Bob, anyway? I didn't know either man well, but Bob seemed perfectly nice. He mostly lived by himself, like me, although he had two kids who stayed with him sometimes. Two boys, elementary school ages. He must have joint custody, which made me suspect he'd been through some hard times with his family. If anything, I felt sorry for him. He was one of those bigger guys who had a much higher voice than you'd expect, which made him seem vulnerable. Not because he was physically weak, or anything like that, but because people might take him less seriously because of it. I got that. I often worried that people might not take me seriously, and I could see why that would be a concern for him.

"So, you say he's in there all the time," the lady officer said to Brent. "He never comes out of the car at all?"

"Never," said Brent. "I think he must be pissing and shitting in there. Excuse my language."

"Uh-huh," said the cop, "and how long has this been going on?"

Brent shook his head. "Hell if I know. I've been smelling it for at least a week."

"Have you spoken to each other?"

I looked back at the other cop, who seemed pretty agitated. I could hear that he was raising his voice, almost yelling, though I couldn't pick out individual words. I was getting really worried about Bob. When I looked at his face through the windshield, though, he seemed relaxed. Smiling, even. Maybe he genuinely wasn't worried, or maybe he was the kind of person who can't stop smiling when they're stressed. I felt an urge to check on him, but I was too nervous to move from where I stood.

"We're advising him that he'll need to clean up the odor," the officer continued. "Have there been any other problems?"

"Isn't there *anything* more you can do?" said Brent. "How am I supposed to sleep with that smell?"

Even though this didn't have anything to do with me, I found myself picking a side. Sure, Bob's car did smell pretty bad, but Brent's reaction seemed extreme. What was he trying to get them to do, throw Bob in jail? Over an odor? The poor guy was probably just too preoccupied to clean the car. Too worried about his kids, maybe.

Brent talked to the other cops for a while, too. Still on my porch. I didn't do much except stand there, and I only did that because I felt like I couldn't leave the porch while they were all on it. After a while, Brent stomped back into his house like an angry toddler and the cops pulled away.

I let out a deep sigh. As I opened my screen door, I glanced over at Bob's little white car. He was still in the driver's seat. Still

THE MOTORIST

smiling. Poor guy, I thought. Probably too scared to move, after that ordeal. I wondered if I should say something, like some words of comfort, but the fact was, I just didn't know him that well.

I had planned to put my lingerie back on after the police left, but now it was all dusty. I'd put it in the vent out of habit, because that was where I used to store all of it, before I worked up the courage to keep it in my closet. Back in those days, though, I would put it in a Ziploc so it didn't get dirty. Now, the thought of putting it back on my body didn't feel sexy at all. I tried reading an old issue of *Cosmo* that I'd found in the trash to get myself back in the mood, but I ended up falling asleep instead.

I was fucking myself in the mirror again. That's weird, I thought, because I couldn't remember getting out of bed, or dressing up. Something felt off, until I noticed that I was also a horse. Ah, okay, I thought, I'm dreaming.

It was not something I would have thought of as fun, when I was awake. But it made me feel amazing. Am I a furry? I wondered. But I wasn't wearing an anthropomorphic horse-person costume; I was definitely an actual horse. Reaching a somehow human ghost-hand that I controlled with my mind down my horse-panties to pleasure myself.

Bob drove his car through the wall of my living room. I couldn't see it happening, as the living room was directly under my bedroom, but I could feel it through the floor.

I didn't want to be a bad host, so I descended the stairs. Thankfully, the living room had already rebuilt the wall behind Bob, whose car was idling on the carpet. My living room now looked like a very small dealership showroom. I had always wondered how they got the cars inside the building for those showrooms, and now I knew.

"Hey," I said.

"Hey," said Bob.

My cat came out from behind the recliner. Bob's car lifted its hood, which contained multiple rows of fiberglass teeth (like a shark) and a timing belt tongue that coiled itself around the cat and snatched it inside the mouth. The hood snapped shut.

"Sorry about your cat," said Bob.

"That's okay," I said, "I don't have a cat."

Gore sprayed from the dashboard vents, spattering a fine, rust-colored mist onto the seats, windows, and Bob's face.

"Not anymore," said Bob. We both laughed. I felt a sense of camaraderie with Bob, in that moment. "I notice you're dressed for the occasion," he said.

He was right: I was still wearing my lacy horse bustier and ruched horse panties. My heart rate spiked.

"Oh god, I'm so sorry," I sputtered, in a voice even higher than Bob's. "I didn't know I was going to have company, you see!"

"Hey, it's okay," said Bob. "It's fine. I'm naked."

I clip-clopped around the car so that I could look through the relatively blood-free windshield. Bob spoke the truth. His bare torso protruded directly from the driver's seat. Its cushion began where his waist ended.

"You *are* naked!" I said. "And you're a centaur!"

"Yes," said Bob, "I am. We're the same, you and I."

"We're both horses!" I wept.

"I accept you," said Bob.

"I accept you, too!" I said.

We hugged. Somehow. I came.

In the morning, I brushed my teeth. I put on sensible, comfortable khakis; sensible, comfortable brown Rockports; and a sensible green button-up. I toasted a bagel, boiled water for instant coffee, peeled a banana. Scrolled through social media. Grabbed my office badge and headed out, as ready for work as I was on any given day.

Bob's Honda was parked right next to my little Focus, with him asleep in the driver's seat. I paused at the passenger window, debating the politics of waking him. My barely-caffeinated brain justified that we had already seen each other as naked horses, and it wasn't until I had already knocked on the window that I remembered that wasn't true at all.

He didn't startle at all, just opened his eyes without moving any other body part. "Hey," he said.

"Uh . . . H-hey," I said.

THE MOTORIST

Bob stretched his arms above his head, elbows bent to avoid hitting the roof. I could see, through the window, that he still had both legs, and was in no way conjoined with the seat. "Off to work, huh?" he said.

"Y-yeah. Off to work." I scratched the back of my neck. "Hey Bob, are you, like, okay? After last night?"

"Oh. Oh, yeah. Some people, you know?" He turned the ignition and the car purred to life, as if stretching its own arms.

"I do," I said. "What is Brent's problem, anyway?"

"Brent?" said Bob. He folded his arms over the crease of his belly, furrowing his eyebrows and sticking out his bottom lip, like a child deep in thought. "Oh, the neighbor guy! Is that who called the police?"

"Didn't they tell you?" I asked.

"I don't remember what they told me," said Bob. He rolled down the window, presumably so that we could talk more clearly. As soon as it cracked, a wave of odor hit me, pressurized inside the car and now being released. "I'll be fine. I really will," he said. "Thanks for your concern, though. It means a lot, these days."

"You headed to work too?" I asked.

"Me? Nah. No work."

I had to admit that the smell pouring out of the car was severe. Still, I didn't get the sense that he was, as Brent had insisted, using the bathroom inside the car. It really did smell more like dog food, a kind of meat-cereal smell. The backseat was littered with fast food wrappers.

"Gotcha," I said. "Well, hey. Let me know if you need anything, okay? I'm here for you, man."

Bob smiled "Thanks, man."

I smiled back.

"Well, see you later," he said.

"Sure." I waved. Got into my car and turned the ignition. Here we are, I thought, just two guys sitting in their cars, getting ready to face the day. We're comrades, I thought. We're on the same team.

Bob rolled out of the lot ahead of me. We wound through the curvy, suburban streets, a little caravan of two. At the main road, he turned right, toward the shopping mall by the outerbelt. I turned left, toward the highway, and watched him going the other way in my rearview.

M.SHAW

At work, the pre-press manager chewed me out for forgetting to convert a page of text that contained the symbol for Planck's Constant to an image, causing the symbol to appear as an italicized lower-case h instead when printed. These things were incredibly important when our main client published scientific journals, she explained, as if I did not know this. It was a miracle that QC had caught it, otherwise we would really have been in hot water. This was a little reassuring, because "hot water" was the phrase she used when I was only kind of in trouble. If I were in big trouble, I would have heard the word "kerfuffle," and that one never came up.

I frequently thought of my and Bob's exchange in the parking lot.

I'm here for you, man.
Thanks, man.
Sometimes I switched who had said what, in my mind.

When I got home, Brent was standing on his porch again, wearing a shirt this time. The shirt said *COLLEGE*.

"Can you believe that dicktard?" he said as I walked toward my door, avoiding eye contact. "Can you believe it?" he repeated. "He's avoiding me. Dicktard."

I went inside my house.

When I reached my bedroom, I realized I had left the blinds open above my bed. Because I had snubbed Brent, and wanted to avoid him seeing me, I took the hand mirror from my bathroom and crept back into the bedroom, on hands and knees, until I was crouching directly below the window. From there, I used the mirror to check if Brent was still outside, and if he was watching for me to appear. He was still there, but he was glaring at the parking lot. Just to be safe, I crawled to the closet, shut myself inside, and stood up to change out of my work clothes.

Now that I was in here, it was actually kind of nice in the closet. Usually, I just treated it as a giant drawer for clothes, but it really was like its own little room. If I wanted, I could bring my laptop in

THE MOTORIST

here, and a chair. Have a private movie night. It smelled of plywood and fabric softener.

On the top shelf, I spotted one of those full-head vinyl horse masks. I had worn it to the office Halloween party four years ago and got big laughs, then stashed it here and forgot about it.

By jumping and grabbing at the mask, I was able to get it down without the step ladder. I picked out something close to the bustier from the dream, a silky black piece with red lace cups. I decided to forego panties and put on a garter belt with some red fishnet stockings, leaving my cock and ass bare.

I crawled back out of the closet. My plan was to take the full-length mirror off the wall and bring it back into the closet with me. Seeing myself on all fours, though, wearing the horse mask with my cock dangling freely, I decided I couldn't help myself. I grabbed the bottle of lube from my bedside table.

I tried to think of horse-related phrases as I slid my hand up and down my shaft. *Working up a lather* came to mind. *I'm working myself into a lather*, I thought, staring at my own vinyl horse eyes.

I jizzed directly onto the carpet, figuring that, at the very least, I'd have to get it cleaned before I moved out.

I Grubhubbed some pad thai for dinner and had time to order a synthetic horse tail butt plug off Amazon before it arrived. Occasionally, throughout the evening, I peeked through the blinds to see if Brent was there. Mostly he wasn't, but sometimes he was, always glaring at the parking lot, like he had been hours earlier. I assumed he was waiting for Bob to come home, so he'd have an excuse to call the police.

On that note, where was Bob? He had said he was okay, but was he really? I felt like he and I were in this together, somehow. I couldn't exactly articulate what "this" was, but we were definitely together in it. I wasn't used to being in anything with anyone, so I was willing to roll with this, even though I was short on specifics.

I played some Halo. On my last check outside, Bob still wasn't back, so I went to bed. It was hard to fall asleep, so I took a melatonin.

Even that didn't quite do it. Desperate, and losing track of which way was up, I tried counting sheep. Eventually, the sheep changed into horses, all spouting the lines I'd been repeating to myself all day. Horses with my and Bob's faces, saying, *I'm here for you, man. Thanks, man.*

Sometimes the horses were also cars.

Bob's car was still idling in my living room. It hadn't moved since the previous dream. I started in my bedroom again, but I knew he was down there because I could smell the exhaust. I knew it was exhaust, even though it didn't have the stale, oily stink that car exhaust normally does. This smell was more organic. Almost meaty. Dog food, I realized.

"Hey," I said when I came downstairs.

"Hey." Bob frowned. "You're not a horse anymore."

"Sorry. I'll try to be." I squeezed my eyes shut and concentrated as hard as I could on being a horse. When I opened my eyes, I was wearing the vinyl mask. "There, see! I *am* a horse!"

"But that's just a mask. I'm a horse forever." His gaze fell pensively to where his waist blended into the upholstery. "I thought we were the same."

"I'm really sorry," I insisted. I was breathing the exhaust directly. It was like having a well-done steak shoved up my sinuses. "We are. I promise. We're in this together."

"Are you sure?" said Bob. "I'm not used to feeling like I'm in anything with anyone. Not even my kids. *Definitely* not my ex." He shook his head. "That's why I like it here so much."

I coughed. "Here? In my house?"

"No," said Bob. "Here, in your dreams."

It was getting difficult to breathe at all. I wanted to take off the mask, but I also didn't want to insult Bob. "Do you think you could turn the engine off?" I said. "Or maybe drive outside?"

"The car won't fit through the door," said Bob. "Besides, I thought I was invited?"

"Please," I choked. "I think I'm dying." It was hard to see much through the mask, but Bob didn't look bothered by the exhaust. He regarded me from inside the car with an expression of vague concern. "Why aren't you dying?" I asked.

THE MOTORIST

"Everyone's dying, Bruce," said Bob. "It just hurts some people more, for longer." In my hazy vision, I could barely see him bounce his head from side to side, as if considering something. "But you know, if we were *really* in this together, you might not have to."

I tried to ask what he meant, but my lungs were full of hotdog vapor.

"Well, you would have to for a little bit, but not for long. Don't worry," said Bob. "I'm here for you, man."

"Really?" I managed to whisper.

Bob didn't respond, because he was dead.

So I died too.

I woke in a melatonin haze, only half-able to make my body obey my brain and only half-able to figure out what I wanted it to do anyway. I wanted to be asleep, but I also wanted to hack up all the car exhaust I'd inhaled. I made it to the bathroom and was retching into the toilet before I realized it had been a dream, and my lungs were fine.

It was the middle of the night, so it made sense that I felt like this. Waking up midway through a sleep cycle after taking melatonin always made me disoriented. I was going to be like this all day.

Going back to sleep, I knew, was a lost cause. At this point, it was a question of what to do until it was time for work. It was 3:32 a.m. I could game for a few hours, but I was also pretty hungry. Ravenous, in fact, like I hadn't eaten in days. I put on a t-shirt and basketball shorts, figuring I could go to a 24-hour diner. I was already thinking about pancakes. Hashbrowns. Bacon. Sausage. Maybe a hamburger. Fried chicken. Honey-baked ham. Bone marrow. Sausage, again. There's a lot of different kinds of sausage. I'd never had blood sausage before and I didn't know exactly what it was, but right now, I'd be willing to give it a shot. Also corned beef. Fried bologna. I had to get to iHop.

Bob's car was back. He was in the driver's seat, wide awake. He waved as I walked toward my Focus, and I waved back. He rolled down the window.

"Hey," he said. "You're up late."

"Hey," I said. "You too."

"You okay?" he asked.

My nostrils flared, taking in the meaty aroma from Bob's car. *He* was asking *me* if *I* was okay? I had assumed he was the one worth worrying about. I thought about it, though. *Was* I okay? I certainly didn't feel okay. Largely because of the melatonin, but not solely.

"I was about to go to iHop," I said. "Want to come?" I blushed when I said *come* and hoped he didn't notice.

"iHop." Bob rubbed his chin. "Do they have a drive-thru?"

"I don't think so."

"Oh well," he sighed.

"It doesn't have to be iHop," I said. "We could go somewhere else that's open late. McDonald's? White Castle? I mean, not that you have to join me, it's just, you seemed disappointed, so, and Brent might call the cops again if he finds out you're here?"

"I could do White Castle," said Bob. "I'll drive, you buy?"

The lock on Bob's passenger door clicked open, and I climbed inside. The seat was clean, but damp, like he had left the window open when it rained. The floor in front of the seat was a ball pit of empty coffee cups. The back seat was no longer exactly a seat, but a shelf for newspapers and dirty clothes. A few plastic grocery bags full of trash sat on the floor, tied shut.

Bob took a bottle of Gatorade from the cup holder, opened his door, and dumped it out on the asphalt. "I'll head to the one on Karl Rd, unless you've got another preference."

I realized the Gatorade bottle had not contained Gatorade. "That's fine," I said. We pulled out of the lot without another word.

The car was silent on the drive to White Castle. We didn't even have the radio on. I struggled to find something to talk about, purely for the sake of comfort.

"So, how are the kids?" I offered.

"I don't know," said Bob. "They're fine, I guess. Didn't see them last week. Or the week before. It's not a custody thing, I just let them stay with their mom. They like it there. And I'm, eh, I'm okay. I'm great, actually. You don't have kids, do you, Bruce?"

"No," I said. "I mean, no, I don't. Not no, I do. I don't have kids." I drummed my hands on my knees. "How's work?"

"It's fine. Look, we're here."

THE MOTORIST

We ordered a sack of 20 sliders. Bob got a Coke. We sat in the parking lot, picking the tiny, oniony-smelling burgers out of the bag and throwing them back like popcorn. Even though they were practically mystery meat, processed to the point of being unrecognizable, they were exactly what I wanted. What I needed.

"Thanks for treating," said Bob. "How's work for you?"

"Oh, you know," I said. "It's work."

"What more can you say."

"Yeah." Wait, I wondered, was he actually asking me to say something more? Dig a little deeper, maybe? We *were* supposed to be in this together, after all. "Hey," I continued, "and I hope I'm not being too forward here, but, like . . . are you *sure* you're okay?"

"Totally sure." Bob chuckled. "Why? What's up?"

"It's just . . . Are you . . . living in your car?"

"Yeah, pretty much," he said. "It's great, actually. You know, you can even charge your phone in these things, now." He gestured to his phone, plugged into the dash. "And I can use the phone as a hotspot, so I even have the internet on my laptop in here. It's not for everyone, I know. Tried to have a slumber party in here with the kids a few weeks ago, but they didn't go for it. That's kinda why they're with their mom all the time now."

He had delivered it all so flatly that I began to suspect I was the one being weird about this. "Don't you miss them?" I said.

"Yeah, of course. I don't think they miss me, though." He unplugged his phone and flipped around on the screen. "Here, look."

The display showed the texts he'd exchanged with his ex. The last one at the bottom read, *Hey, are you coming to get the kids today?* It was almost three weeks old.

"I never responded, and I haven't heard anything since," he said. "So I guess no one's too upset."

I peeked into the burger bag, eager to diffuse the tension I felt building. There were three sliders left. "I think I've had about ten," I said. "How many have you had?"

"Twelve," said Bob.

"Huh, they must have given us extra." I plucked another one out, grateful for the luck. I didn't feel even a little bit full. "Do you ever leave the car?" I said between bites.

"Don't need to," said Bob. "Don't worry, though, it's not like I'm fused to the seat, or anything." He took another slider himself.

"Thank goodness." I took the last one. It seemed equitable. I caught myself in a moment of revulsion at the idea of him never leaving the car, but then I remembered that Brent was the real bad guy, here. Bob living in his car might be weird, sure, but he wasn't hurting anybody. It was just a lifestyle choice.

Besides, we were in this together.

"Hey," I said, "should we clean this thing out a little, before we go back?"

"This . . . thing?" said Bob.

"The car," I clarified. "To keep Brent from calling the police again."

"You think he would?" said Bob.

"He definitely would," I said. "He's obsessed."

"Wow," said Bob. "Well . . . okay. I guess it couldn't hurt."

Bob pulled up to the concrete trash enclosure at the back of the parking lot, and I offloaded the trash bags directly from the backseat, tossing them one-by-one over the lip of the Dumpster. "It could use a vacuum," I said, as I tossed the last of it.

"If we go get one from Walmart, I can run it in the car," said Bob. "There's an outlet in the console that I use for my laptop."

The nearest Walmart was a little farther away, but then, it was still just before 5:00. If I went home now, I'd have an hour to kill before I could justify getting ready for work. I agreed to tag along.

At Walmart, Bob gave me his credit card and sat in the back of the lot while I went in. A greeter nodded to me, rubbing at eyes that were nearly swollen shut. Watching him made me realize how raw my own eyes felt, though I hadn't been rubbing at them.

"Hey," a familiar voice said behind me as I stared vacantly at shelves of cleaning products.

"Bob?" I turned.

"Eww, no," said Brent. "No, I'm not Bob. Jesus. If I were Bob, you'd smell me coming. And hear me, since he never leaves that damn car."

My stomach knotted. If I'd known Brent were here, I would have made an effort to avoid him. It wasn't just how he treated Bob; we'd hung out a few times, right after I moved into the

THE MOTORIST

complex, but then once he'd said some pretty insensitive things about transgender people and I hadn't been comfortable with him since. I didn't even understand why, because I wasn't a transgender person, I just liked wearing the clothes, and thinking about that just made me even more uncomfortable.

"What are you doing here so early?" I asked. I plucked a vacuum off the shelf, suddenly clear-minded about choosing one and getting out.

"Eh," said Brent. "Nothing else to do. They cut my hours at work and my schedule's all fucked up. Plus my girlfriend left. Bitch."

"Sorry to hear it," I said.

"Not that I care," said Brent. "Good riddance."

Had he come up to me just to say that? I hadn't known his girlfriend, and only saw her once or twice, and I couldn't imagine what she could have done to justify his language.

"How about you?" he said. "What brings you here in the wee hours? You're not helping Bob, are you?"

"Helping . . . ?" I stammered. "N-no. Why would you think that?"

Brent shook his head. "He's always getting people to do all this weird shit for him, so he doesn't have to leave his car. Me and him, we used to be friends. But then he kept needing me to, like, grocery shop for him. Once he demanded I bring him a bucket of water and a towel, so he could bathe. In his fucking car. I was like, no, that's disgusting, I'm not fucking doing that. Then he begged, and I still said no, and he told me if I was really his friend I'd do it, and then he said it'd be a shame if anything happened to my girlfriend, and that's where I draw the damn line with people like him. Makes it that much worse now that she's actually gone."

My legs refused to move while Brent was talking. This must have been some intense stuff for him, and it seemed like I should listen, even if I didn't like him much. I was sure he must be making up the parts about how Bob talked to him, or, at least, he wasn't telling the whole story.

"Listen," he said. "Bob. He's a bad guy. I know you've been talking to him. He knows how to act nice, but trust me. He's up to some bad shit."

"How do you know?" I said.

"I know."

"Okay," I said. "I have to pay for my vacuum now."

I ducked into the closest available checkout lane, leaving him in front of the produce section with a cart full of Keystone and Spaghetti-O's.

"I'll wash the clothes," I said, gesturing to the pile in the backseat when we pulled back into the complex. "Should be time before work." Maybe I was taking on a lot for Bob, but I still felt sorry for the guy. And I wanted him to like me. I wanted us to be there for each other, like we'd said. Also, I didn't want to give Brent the satisfaction of getting to call the cops.

I ran and grabbed the Febreeze from my kitchen. "Brent was complaining about the smell," I explained, spraying down the car's interior. I wasn't sure how to tell Bob that he needed a shower as well, so I just made sure to spray him, too, from an angle where it looked like I was getting him on accident.

"Thanks, Bruce. Hey, do me one more favor?" He worked a key off his keyring, still dangling from the ignition. "Can you check on my cat?"

"Sure thing, Bob." I accepted the key.

"Want the rest of these?" He handed me the slider bag. I was sure we'd eaten them all, but when I looked inside, there were four left. Imagine that, I thought. "Great. Fantastic!" He grinned, face glistening with Febreeze. "Enjoy work."

"Thanks. Uh, see you later, man."

He drove off. I threw the dirty clothes in the wash, and got ready for work.

I was still hungry, so I had the sliders for breakfast. Something about the thin burger patties tasted wrong. Still greasy, but too dry and bland, like they were full of saw dust. Almost like . . . "Dog food?" I whispered. I opened the bun of the one I was eating. Prodded the patty with my finger. No, it was just as spongy and meaty in texture as it should be. I shrugged, and finished the bag.

THE MOTORIST

At work, it turned out a major client had dropped our contract. The one with the physics books. I had to dig out our archive of their journals, which went back to 1997, on a series of CD-RW's in an old Xerox paper box. I had to scratch up the bottom of each one with a screwdriver and throw them away. As this client represented 40% of the company's workload, it also meant I would be on unpaid leave all next week.

I ate lunch in my car. It felt like a better place to be than the break room. Plus, as I'd suspected, I had sliders again. The taste was really growing on me.

I went into Bob's apartment as soon as I got home. Bob wasn't there, of course. Nobody was. At first, I couldn't open the door, but a firm nudge with my shoulder finally got it free of the frame. As if the door had started to fuse itself shut from disuse.

Bob's townhouse looked a lot like mine. The buildings had different landlords, but they all used the same cheap, brown carpeting, same off-white semigloss paint, same flimsy light fixtures. The biggest difference I could see was that Bob had a couch instead of a recliner, which made sense, him having kids.

The cat's bowl and litter box were in the bathroom at the top of the stairs. The litter box was badly over-filled, such that the cat had abandoned it and was going on the floor. Its water was empty, but the food dish, somehow, was mostly full. Although, judging from the way the bathroom smelled, this particular food had also been sitting out for a few days.

I emptied the litter box into the toilet, a few scoops at a time, flushing periodically so it wouldn't clog. I wiped up the stuff on the floor with toilet paper. I refilled the water dish, but I didn't see a fresh bag of litter anywhere, so I made a mental note to remind Bob next time I saw him. The cat could make do somehow until then.

Come to think of it, I realized that I hadn't actually seen a cat anywhere. I thought I'd better have a look around, to make sure it hadn't gotten out.

I swept through the kitchen and living room, checking in cupboards and behind furniture. I went back upstairs and checked the kids' bedroom, then across the hall to Bob's room.

M.SHAW

I felt dizzy. Bob's room looked *exactly* like my room. Not that it was the exact same furniture, or anything like that, but the layout. Queen size bed, small bedside table with a desk lamp, dresser in one corner, full-length mirror in the other corner with a little rug in front of it. The same proportions. There was nothing objectively unusual about any of it, but it was all in the exact same spot, like a Mirror World version of my room.

"Here, kitty," I chanted, looking under the bed, checking all the nooks and crannies like I had in the other rooms. The closet door was open a crack, so I checked in there.

On the hangers, women's lingerie. More expensive than the stuff in my closet. My eye settled on a matching set whose fabric was patterned like Delft pottery. I imagined how it would feel to wear it; how I would feel so delicate, and rare, and precious.

Bob wasn't going to be coming back inside anytime soon, was he?

After I put it on, I decided I had to find the cat before I did anything else. I had to help Bob, like I promised. Besides, delayed gratification would make the payoff all the more satisfying.

The only place I hadn't checked was the basement. I slipped on a set of white pumps I found on the over-the-door shoe rack.

There was a car in the basement. A 90's Civic. The entire thing. Just sitting on the floor, like it was a dealership showroom. How had Bob gotten it down here? Somebody would have had to disassemble it, move it down piece-by-piece, and then reassemble the whole thing. It must have been down here for a long time, because I didn't remember seeing an operation like that going on in the complex.

I walked around the Civic, heels clip-clopping on the cement floor. Unlike Bob's Fit, this car was clean inside, except for the film of dust that covered everything. I sat down in the back seat.

The interior smelled like sweat gone stale. Like an old pair of shoes. It was not a pleasant car to sit in, and I found that this fact carried a transgressive sort of thrill. This was a dirty, unkempt car. Sitting there, I felt like the car's miasma would soil me, or anyone who got inside.

I laid down. Imagined being taken back here. By someone with a grill for a mouth, headlights for eyes. Wearing a varsity jacket with a Honda logo where the letter should be. With breath that revved like an engine. I came.

Then the police did.

THE MOTORIST

Brent had reported me for breaking and entering, when he saw me nudge open the door with my shoulder. At least, that's what I managed to gather in the haze of humiliation and questioning that ensued as I lay in the back seat of the Civic. I had left the front door cracked open, so they could enter without a warrant.

I didn't get arrested. I showed them the key Bob had given me, and they called him to confirm he'd asked me to be there. Most of them took photos of me with their phones.

Nobody asked what the car was doing in the basement.

That night, I dreamed about the Disney movie *Pocahontas*. Well, the dream wasn't *about* the movie, it just *was* the movie, start to finish. Except Pocahontas was driving a garbage truck in every shot. She drove the garbage truck off the waterfall and careened into the lake below, sang "Colors of the Wind" while tearing through the woods in the garbage truck, drove the garbage truck in front of her father to save John Smith's life. There was one added scene, a prolonged overhead shot of the multi-point turn she had to make out of Grandmother Willow's grove.

I would rather not have woken up.

I spent most of the following day in bed. I called the office first thing, to ask if they needed me. They didn't. So I crawled back under the covers, setting an alarm for 11 o'clock so I could call in a delivery from Pizza Hut when they opened. A big enough pizza would feed me for the entire day, and I wouldn't have to worry about leaving the bed again. Normally I would get one with veggies on it, so it was at least a little bit healthy, but I wasn't in the mood for pretending. Today, I could get a meat lover's. Maybe even with no cheese or sauce, just meat. Extra meat.

The past few days had left me with a lot of uncertainty, but one thing I was sure of was that my life was definitely ending. My secret was out, and it wasn't okay after all. It was shameful, and sad, and there were probably photos of me in Bob's lingerie, with semen in my belly button, being circulated in some secret Facebook group for cops. I had the feeling I was going to keep having to call in to see if I had work each day, and the answer was going to keep being no.

I slept through the alarm. I didn't dream. I woke up at night, starving. Thinking about a car that was also a meat grinder, churning out an endless supply of sausage as it tore over roads that smelled like iron and feces.

I found Bob in the parking lot of the bowling alley on Cleveland Ave, just before midnight. I'd been driving around for hours, looking for a BLD-7178 license plate on a white Honda Fit. He had a takeout bag from Rally's and was sipping out of the biggest soda cup I'd seen anyone hold in a single hand.

"Hey, man," he said, staring through his windshield, at the door of the bowling alley.

"Hey, man," I said. "Got your clothes. All clean."

"Thanks. That's really thoughtful of you."

I opened the passenger door and sat down next to him. The dry, meaty smell was already starting to seep through the Febreeze. I looked into the Rally's bag and saw that there was an entire Big Buford inside, still in the paper. "You gonna eat that?"

"Nah," said Bob. "That one's for you. I got an extra."

I had been to McDonald's while I was driving around, but I got to work on the burger without another word.

"This might be an odd question," I said, "but if I looked inside that Rally's bag right now, would there be another Big Buford in it?"

"There might."

"How does that work?" I asked.

"I come here sometimes," said Bob. "It's a good place. Lots of people coming and going. Easy to just blend in. Be one more car in the lot. The people watching is great."

I didn't respond because I was busy eating.

"You ever read that book *Bowling Alone*?" said Bob.

THE MOTORIST

I shook my head.

"Yeah, me either. Not much of a reader. But the title gave me the idea to do this." He took another long draw on his soda, then put it down and pointed at a man in a checkered polo coming out of the bowling alley. "Take this guy. Showed up by himself about 45 minutes ago. Leaving by himself now. Watch, he's in the green Infiniti by the lamp post in the next row."

The man walked halfway down the row of cars, then folded himself into the sedan Bob had indicated.

"He's all by himself," said Bob. "Probably by himself wherever he's going, too. Want to find out where that is?"

I wondered if Bob was thinking what I was thinking: that the guy getting into the Infiniti didn't have anyone who was there for him, the way Bob and I were for each other.

"What are we gonna do once we find out?" I asked.

"We'll take him with us," said Bob. "Up to the dog food factory, north of town. You know the one."

"In the middle of the night?"

"There's people there at night," he said. "People like us. People who need to keep their doggy bag full. All my friends are there, you should come."

I blushed a little, hearing Bob say "come." I breathed deep. The smell of his car was oddly comforting, now. It helped me think. Helped me consider options I hadn't considered before.

"And after that," I said, "do you think we could . . . take Brent . . . to the dog food factory?"

Bob shook his head. "Brent's got a girlfriend. You've gotta watch that stuff. He's not alone. Too easy to miss."

"He is now," I said. "His girlfriend left."

"No kidding." Bob grinned. I'd never seen him grin. "Let's talk about that tomorrow night. Now, we gonna follow this guy, or what?"

I swallowed the last chunks of white bread and beef. "You know, why not?" I said. "We're in this together, man."

"That's what I like to hear," said Bob. "I'll follow him, you follow me?"

I got back into my silver Focus. My laptop charger blinked on when I turned the ignition, as did the charging light on my phone. The suitcase full of my clothes sat neatly in the back seat.

We pulled out of the lot.

M.SHAW

During the days, I dream about tar. Bitumen. Bubbling up out of the earth like acid reflux. Asphalt being mixed and poured. Fossil fuel. The food we all become, sooner or later.

I dream about blood drying between tire treads. Mixing with the road grime, forming into something between blood sausage and concrete. I dream about those tires rolling over the grid of digestive juices that covers the world, just for us to move across.

At night, we hunt. Four wheels make you so much faster than two legs. And you blend right in. 300 million people on the roads, just trying to keep the tank full. The refineries never go hungry, and neither do we.

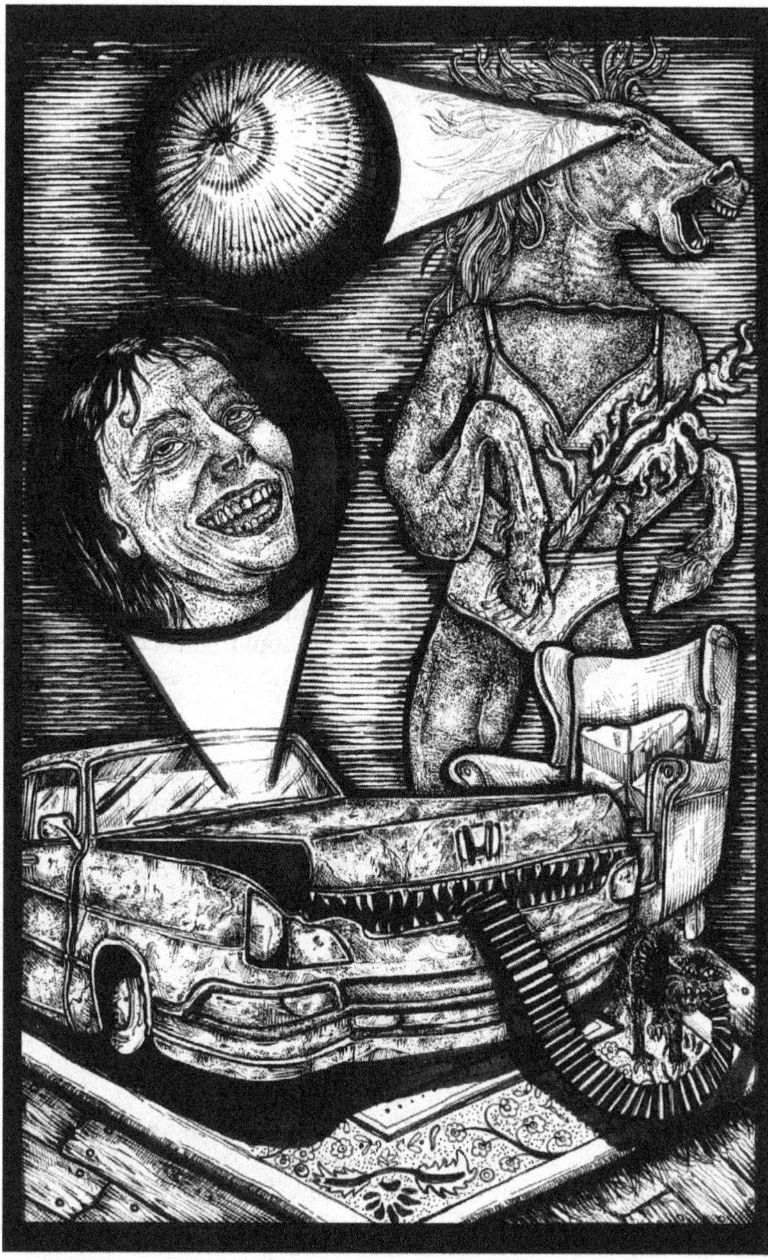

MAN VS. BOMB

WATCH. The starter pistol sounds. The man takes off running. Five seconds later, the bomb takes off after him. The man is young and strong, for a human, but his legs are short. He's naked and doesn't have much hair, even on top of his head. His genitals swing frantically, like a smaller, more terrified version of him, as he runs from the bomb.

The bomb is visibly less ashamed of his nakedness. He freely displays his many open sores, his exposed rib cage where the flesh was chewed away by the bomb that caught him yesterday, when he was the man. He pursues today's man without malice, only hunger. Behind his ribs, you can see some of the prize money stuffed between his remaining organs.

This transformation is the most beautiful thing about the race. Even if the bomb explodes before he catches the man, the man will never get back what he believes is his by right. The man craves his lost ability to dominate the world through force and industry, but the forest people have taken this from him. The bomb craves only skin and sinew between his teeth. He is closer to his roots as an animal, a purer kind of human than the man, and, as such, he has already won.

The deer packed into the stands cheer on one contestant or the other as they circle the track. The man keeps looking over his shoulder. He refuses to resist the urge. Every time he strains his body to check the bomb's progress, the distance between them shortens. He keeps forgetting that all he has to do to win is run, and nothing else, for long enough to beat the bomb's timer.

You will have to understand this, too. To survive the race, you have to learn to think like the prey animal that the new world has

MAN VS. BOMB

made of you. To watch like prey, listen like prey, breathe like prey. To repeat this pattern until you no longer can. To let go of the idea that you will ever stop running.

The man turns to fight. Another common mistake. He throws a punch and misses, his motor control shot by his terror. The bomb tackles him and sinks his teeth in, ripping flesh from the man's face, from his torso, from his throat. The man's limbs flail under the bomb's weight, until they stop. He relaxes. Falls silent. His eyes glaze. He is already ceasing to think about anything more than his desire to feed. He will not even need to sleep or mate anymore, after this. He is being wiped clean; renewed, and, in his renewal, ready at last to be part of a civilized world.

The bomb explodes, a series of muffled pops from the small charges planted along his spine, littering the track with the money sewn into his body cavity. Paper bills shower the man as he lies, uncaring, on the ground. The deer in the audience celebrate, or swear and rip up their tickets. The man is unaffected. The handlers come to collect him, scooping him up by the shoulders with their antlers. They help him into the stable where he will spend the night.

He will be your bomb.

Listen.

You are a criminal. Understand this, above all else. Asking what crime you have committed is almost beside the point. You're a human in a deer's world; it would be more apt to ask what crime you haven't committed. You have taken what is not yours, you have destroyed what you cannot keep. You have murdered, and devoured your kill without respect to the sanctity of the hunt.

But we are not cruel, like you. We believe everyone deserves a second chance; the race is yours. You will be judged by the criteria that your kind always applied to us: survival of the fittest. Just be aware, fitness, for you, no longer looks the way you think it does.

And so you find yourself here, tethered in the stable. As your trainer, it's my responsibility to prepare you for the race tomorrow. I hope you'll take what I've shown you in the video to heart. You may not believe I want you to win, but I do. I take pride in my reputation, and that's why I've told you everything I'm allowed about what to expect. I've also made sure that your needs are taken care of. Here, in the stable, you'll be fed in accordance with your dietary needs. You'll be allowed to bathe, to clothe yourself until you are stripped bare for the race tomorrow. You have a safe place to sleep, which, I imagine, is a welcome relief from being out in the world at large, constantly fighting other humans over the scraps of your dead society. Isn't it nice, knowing that tonight, at least, you are safe?

Do you remember the world before the forest people rose up? I don't, of course. Even with all the benefits of medical science, deer only live 25, maybe 30 years. But your kind live much longer, even without the aid of all that technology. I'm only 10 myself, but you, if I understand human aging correctly, you must have been an adult before it happened. Maybe you even hunted us. Maybe you had a stuffed head on your wall. Maybe you and all your friends once sat in a blind not far from here, eagerly awaiting *your* sport. If so, I don't hold it against you. Our relationship is purely that of a trainer and his charge. I think nothing of you outside the context of the race, and neither should you.

I leave you to yourself for the evening, though I can still observe you on the stable cameras. I need to take note of your behavior, to see if you need any more instruction tomorrow morning. Often, captured men are tempted to try to escape, or stay up all night, consumed with anxiety, in some sad attempt to make sense of their situation.

Not you, though. You eat your dinner, clean yourself, and then lay on your bed of straw. Good. You should get as much rest as you can. If you do this well, you'll wake with your mind fresh, rid of any illusions of meaning. The brain can only handle so much activity at once, and you'll want to spend it all on moving your legs. For the rest of your life, until you can't anymore. My expectations are high.

Breathe.

The starter pistol sounds. You take off running. Five seconds later, the bomb takes off after you. The bomb who was the young, short-legged man yesterday. You have the advantage in stride, at least. Here's to finding out if you take it for granted.

MAN VS. BOMB

You certainly run like someone intimately acquainted with what it means to be a prey species. No looking back, no temptation to confront your pursuer. I really get the sense that you understand: being prey is neither as difficult, nor as complicated as your kind tend to think of it. All you do is run.

The bomb, of course, understands what it means to be a predator. He pursues you with complete single-mindedness. He doesn't try to outsmart you, sensing that he can rely on your fear and your exhaustion to do it for him. The bomb doesn't think of himself as a bomb. He doesn't even really think of himself as a hunter. In his mind, there is only his hunger, and you, and a straight line connecting them.

You make one full lap around the track, then another. By the third lap, the air is thick with the dust you've both kicked up. Coming around the curve, you see that hurdles have been set across the track while you were on the other side. I wasn't allowed to warn you about this, and I can see in the momentary slowing of your pace, the swing of your arms, that you're letting your feelings of betrayal penetrate the purified mental state that we worked so hard on yesterday. The line between you and the bomb shortens.

Just in time, you launch yourself toward the first row of hurdles. Jump, and over. The second row of hurdles. Jump, and over.

As you clear the third hurdle, the bomb collides into the first. His body crashes clean through, wood snapping as splinters fly. This is where most men turn and look, if they made it this far. And here, you finally do.

So few of your kind are willing to let go, when it comes down to survival. You have to hold on to the delusion that you are still in control of the world. As if by divine right. This is why you look. You cannot relinquish your entitlement, even when refusing to do so would kill you—and I'm afraid it will.

You pick up the hurdle in front of you and swing it in a wide arc, smashing it across the bomb's shoulder and knocking him on his side. It won't matter. He'll recover from the fall quicker than you will from delivering the blow. You rush over the remaining hurdles, but he catches you by the ankle as you clear the last one.

You both fall. Your head recoils when it smacks, face-first, into the earth. The bomb's arm tangles in the hurdle, breaking the bones of his forelimb. But then, he only needs one hand to catch you.

You manage to slip your leg out of his grip, kicking off into a renewed sprint. You even manage to make it a few steps before he tackles you again, with his remaining arm around your waist.

From my seat next to the announcers' box, with the other trainers, I see your fingers sink into the dirt. Your elbows brace, trying to pull your prone body forward. To draw out the line between predator and prey by just a few more inches, a few more fractions of a second before the end. The bomb's head strains forward, teeth bared.

The bomb explodes. When you hear the pops, your face plunges into the dirt, believing, I imagine, that the sound means death for you, that the sudden, searing pain in your leg is from a bite, not the explosives. You lie, trembling from the adrenaline dump, as a roar goes up from the stands, the losers and the ones who are still in it, tickets clenched in the clefts of hooves. Bills flutter to the ground around you, onto your back.

The other trainers nod to me. I nod back, swinging my antlers in their own small victory lap. I'm proud of you, in this moment. It was giving in to instinct that saved you, your willingness to rush and scrabble and strive for your life until the very last moment. That is the prey mentality, and you've taken it to heart. We can all see that, now.

Moments pass, and you begin to realize that you are still alive. You stagger upright. Hobble a few steps on your burned leg. It's painful, but you can get around. You take in the sight of the cash littered at your feet.

Nearby, the door back into the stable opens. You can leave the track anytime now, and this is the moment when we will see if you really are a winner, or just another bomb waiting to happen. A canny prey animal would abandon the money, too eager to escape the kill site to give it so much as a second look. A man, on the other hand, would foolishly hold on to the idea that the money is why he is here. He would gather up as much as he could, dreaming of the control it once afforded him over the things he desires, of buying shelter, or weapons, or food, or sex. A man would dare to believe that mere escape is less than the best-case scenario.

At the other end of the track, another door opens. If you are

MAN VS. BOMB

paying attention, you should already be able to intuit what is waiting to be released, just beyond the threshold. The deer in the stands who haven't lost yet hold their tickets close, waiting to see what you will do. If you will survive in fear, or die in ignorance.
    Watch.
    Listen.
    Breathe.

ONE LONG STAIRCASE, JUST GOING UP

THE ALIENS GATHER The 500 Richest Earth Men together in an auditorium.

Listen, they say, your planet is dying. Maybe not in your generation, but it's all going on. Melting ice caps, ocean acidification, all the hits. But that's okay!

It is? say The 500 Richest Earth Men.

Sure! say the aliens. We're here to help! Just sign over what remains of the planet's natural resources to us. We'll send a starship to bring all of you Home. On our planet, you'll enjoy all the luxuries you're accustomed to: mansions! Cars! Space Pussy! Burning Man! You'll never have to worry about any of this again! Just leave the planet in our caring, expert custody, and all this can be yours! No need to answer now, we'll give you time to think it over.

The 500 Richest Earth Men confer, in the world's largest, gold-plated conference room. The planet *is* dying, this they know. But can the aliens be trusted? Who can say whether their motives are pure? Maybe they just want to capture these men, so they can experiment on The 500 Richest Earth Brains.

We do have the best brains, they say. Who wouldn't want a chance to learn about us?

We didn't get to be The 500 Richest Earth Men by taking just any deal that slides our way across God's desk! they say back to themselves. What's these aliens' game? What do they want?

Everybody Wants Something, they all agree. All of them know this: Everybody Wants Something.

The 500 Richest Earth Men play golf with the aliens. The aliens have golf on their homeworld, but they play poorly because they

ONE LONG STAIRCASE JUST GOING UP

are not used to Earth's gravity. The 500 Richest Earth Men's confidence is bolstered. These aliens are good guys! they agree.

The aliens screen a documentary about their homeworld, A Meritocratic Utopia (which is also the name of the documentary). Much like your own planet, says a buttery-voiced alien narrator, the galaxy is filled with underperforming whiners. Except on our world, a Meritocratic Utopia. Here, a man's wealth is defined solely by his merit, and his merit is defined solely by his wealth. Just like you! That's why we're inviting you to join us: because you belong. Here. With all your friends. In a true Meritocratic Utopia.

A Meritocratic Utopia, The 500 Richest Earth Men mumble to each other, their mouths filling with saliva.

The aliens throw a party for The 500 Richest Earth Men, where Space Coke flows freely, as a sample of what awaits them. The party is held inside an abandoned corporate headquarters shaped like a giant picnic basket. On the dance floor, The 500 Richest Earth Men sneak furtive glances at each other, before pairing off and sneaking into the empty offices. In the dark, they pull out their phones and show each other their net worth. Read off emails they've received from the politicians they've bought. Pull markers out of desks and draw lines all over each others' designer business suits. A few have drivers pick them up after midnight, but most of them spend the night in the loading dock, huddled together in an Armani cuddle puddle, surrounded by old baskets.

These aliens get us, they all agree as they scrape themselves up the next morning. Real deal-makers. The Earth will be in good hands.

The 500 Richest Earth Men call a meeting. Will we be able to visit Earth after we leave? they ask the aliens.

Oh my, no! the aliens laugh. Oh goodness gracious no, most certainly not! Their hocks of laughter roar up in unison, like an engine revving. That's not going to be possible *at all!*

The 500 Richest Earth Men can tell there is something the aliens aren't telling them, something sinister about what they intend to do with the Earth once the paperwork is signed. But The 500 Richest Earth Men laugh along. They're all on the same page, here.

All of this is hidden from us, The 8 Billion Poorest Earth People. We don't even know that there are any aliens, although we do know about the dying planet thing. Some blame The 500 Richest Earth Men, while others think The 500 Richest Earth Men will save us. Some even believe both at once.

The 500 Richest Earth Men know this about us, and it fills them with smug contempt. This is exactly why we deserve to be the ones who survive and profit from the final days of Earth, they all agree.

Survive and Profit, they repeat, rubbing their pocket watches like prayer beads. Survive and Profit.

We're not like the 8 Billion Poorest Earth People, they say. We're the deal-makers. The Earth was always ours to take or leave.

There's a reason nobody talks about the 8 Billion Richest Earth Men, they agree.

All of the relevant paperwork is signed. All of the relevant appendages are shaken.

Two weeks later, The 500 Richest Earth Men pile onto the starship that arrives for them. They marvel at the sleekness of its design, like a golf bag. A golf bag sized for a god, with giant, plasma-spewing engines instead of clubs. The inside looks like if an entire 747 were all the first class section, and also a palace in a Disney movie. This is better than Air Force One! they say. There are tiny robots in French maid outfits, who serve brightly-colored cocktails that taste so strongly of nostalgia that it's hard to tell there's any alcohol in them. There are no aliens aboard.

It must be piloted remotely, they assure themselves.

It's probably all app-based, like Uber, they agree.

Their gold-plated ark sails out of Earth's atmosphere, firing on all clubs. On the way out, they pass a fleet of other ships, so black against the void of outer space that they are visible only as an absence of stars. The 500 Richest Earth Men squint at the ships, trying, at least, to discern their outline. Something like a lobster cracker.

If you look to your left, says a gentle, maternal, disembodied voice, you'll just be able to see some of our hard working Planet Juicers. They're here to repurpose your planet's natural resources into the most efficient form possible: Planet Juice! The fuel that drives the entire galactic hegemony, of which you are now a precious, valued, virtually microscopic piece. You will also see the Planet Juicers if you look to the right, or anywhere else.

ONE LONG STAIRCASE JUST GOING UP

The Planet Juicers begin their work. The first thing they juice is The 8 Billion Poorest Earth People, wherever we happen to be: in bed, at work, at school, on the toilet. All we can do is gaze upward at the distinct spatial lack in the sky, feeling the unexplained pressure exerted on us, popping our eardrums at first, then pushing our breath back down our throats, grinding our joints into a paste of bone meal and blood. We are squeezed until we are empty, forcing our mouths open into a gaping O, like the rind of an orange cut in half. Like a tennis ball slit open, pressed between two fingers. We look like we have all just come to an amazing realization. Like we are reaching out, toward one last door-busting deal.

Hey-o! say The 500 Richest Earth Men, watching through the windows of their Space Uber. Look at those Planet Juicers juice!

Before long there is nothing left of the Earth but a dessicated, carbon-based husk. Even that will disappear in a few days, without enough gravity to hold it together. Or what would be a few days, if days existed anymore.

Well, this sucks, says The Moon, who goes off to hang out with Pluto and Eris.

Their tanks full, the Planet Juicers begin their journey back to TK-197, which is not the aliens' homeworld, but a sterile, empty planet that they use to store emergency reserves of Planet Juice. The Earth will not even be filling an immediate need. It is what the aliens, in their language, would call something that translates roughly to "the externalized cost of a generation's inefficacy," or what we might call a "rainy day fund."

The 500 Richest Earth Men clink their martinis together and relax into the seats of their remotely piloted Space Uber.

The aliens, for context, have hundreds of these Space Ubers all over the galaxy. All of them are controlled from EF-898, which is also not the aliens' homeworld. The pilots are two brothers named Chobvanabolmaro and Siobvanabolmaro, who are a different kind of alien from the ones The 500 Richest Earth Men are acquainted with. They have done this job for what we would consider to be about 200 years. The brothers are photosynthetic, with their sleep cycle governed by the presence or absence of daylight. Since EF-898 doesn't have night, they have been awake the entire time.

M. SHAW

On the day The 500 Richest Earth Men's ship embarks, they have had just about enough of this arrangement.

You know what, Chobvanabolmaro? says Siobvanabolmaro.

What is it, Siobvanabolmaro? says Chobvanabolmaro.

Fuck this, says Siobvanabolmaro.

They are vaporized by the guard robots the moment they step outside the control room. They knew this would happen, and were at peace with it. Their planet was juiced eons ago, when their parents made the same deal as The 500 Richest Earth Men, and now they are the last of their species.

Sometimes enough is enough, says Chobvanabolmaro, dissolving into a cloud of ions.

Enough is enough, Siobvanabolmaro tries to say, but can't, because he's dead.

Thanks to the brothers' defection, The 500 Richest Earth Men's ship does not set off on the correct course, for HH-116 (which is *also* not the aliens' homeworld, but a kind of Carnival Cruises planet for former residents of juice planets). Instead, the ship continues in a straight line, directly toward The Sun.

As The 500 Richest Earth Men careen into the exploding ball of gas, they peer through the windows and into its fire, until their retinas burn away completely from the pure heat-light of fusing hydrogen. In one last flash of white-hot brightness, they see the gaping mouths of The 8 Billion Poorest Earth People opening toward them. The Sun is made of our bodies, reaching out. They are falling into our mouths. They are, at last, filling us.

Oh, great, say The 500 Richest Earth Men, here they are again. All the mouths.

They have seen this vision before. They have dreamed about it every night, as long as they can remember. It terrified them when they were young, but slowly grew used to it, until it became merely annoying. The image is so familiar that nearly any mundane, day-to-day stimulus can trigger its memory—the smell of gasoline, the sound of a phone ringing, a financial statement—rendering their world an endless field of insatiable mouths that they spend every breath refusing to feed.

Everybody Wants Something, they say.

They all do, The 500 Richest Earth Men agree. They all want

ONE LONG STAIRCASE JUST GOING UP

something. It doesn't matter how much you give them, all they want is more, more, more.

Sometimes, they say, it feels like all we do is give, give, give.

Give, give, give, they repeat, plummeting into The Sun. They are incinerated, unseeing, in too brief a moment for their bodies to feel. They are spared from pain, from the knowledge that they are disappearing. The aliens have given them this gift, at least: that they will never be confronted with their demise. That their minds will only ever know themselves as The 500 Richest Earth Men, the deal-makers, the last and best scions of Earth. And that they are, for one fleeting instant, unequivocally the best and brightest humanity has to offer.

It took the destruction of an entire world, for them to finally be this free, but it was, as with all earthly bargains, a price they were able to pay. And if this is not what it truly means, to be a Rich Man.

THE ONLY FRIEND YOU EVER NEED

WELL, IT WAS basically my fault for telling Inillustrable Girl she was cute. In my defense, I was only trying to avoid getting on the bad side of the local malak, which at the time was something you had to watch. Of course, conventional wisdom would have said I should never get involved with a malak in the first place, but in this situation, I didn't have that option. She involved herself with me. After that, I could only do my best with what I had.

This happened while I was out jogging one morning. The park was empty, which should have warned me that she might be around, but I had been out late with my—I guess—girlfriend Siobhan the previous night, and I hadn't had my coffee yet and just wasn't that alert. I didn't figure out what was going on until I came to the park and saw her working on her latest victim, which she had already done to the point where I couldn't tell if it had been male or female. She had it strung up from a dead tree in a way that suggested a cubist scarecrow, shoved sticks halfway into all of its joints and was now working on flaying its skin off with a little heat ray that came out of her fingernail.

I'd heard about that heat ray. I had nightmares about her heat ray.

So naturally I tried not to draw any attention to myself. Just keep jogging, I thought, avoid eye contact. Not that avoiding malaks at all cost would necessarily save me or anyone from a gruesome, humiliating death at one's hands, but you have to do what you can. This part of the path took me through the playground, though, and when I came around a bend she was sitting right there in the sandbox, facing me head-on.

THE ONLY FRIEND YOU EVER NEED

I froze. Because I knew I was dead, right? Malaks don't come up to people in public to meet and greet.

I said, "Hello there."

She sort of lolled forward like a nod.

I know that trying to talk my way out of it sounds ridiculous in retrospect. If it helps, remember that I was delirious with lack of sleep. And fear.

Inillustrable Girl, if you don't know, was a shape-changer. This particular day she was being a teenage girl with a floating bucket for a head. The bucket had a fluorescent pink skull sans-jawbone stenciled on, and it *was* cute in a goofy sort of way. So I told her so. Flattery. Her clothes looked exactly like she had pulled them out of a dumpster and slapped them with a coat of neon green spray-paint, and that was less endearing, but I would not have liked to say that out loud.

Everything I said, she just kept doing that nodding thing. I said, "Lovely weather, isn't it?" I thought it was. I said, "How's work?" though it made me shiver. I said, "Well, it was nice seeing you." I kept jogging. By this point, *most* of my organs were in my throat.

She followed me home. I would catch sight of her now and then as I made my way back. I was muttering the last rites to myself when I walked in the door to my townhouse, only to find her sitting on my kitchen table.

I wet myself. I don't mind talking about it. I have nothing to hide, just want to be perfectly honest here.

I said, "What a pleasant surprise! I didn't know you were coming over."

Nod.

I said, "Excuse me, I have to go change."

She didn't follow me upstairs, but she didn't leave. I took a five-minute shower, most of which was spent washing my legs. Then I brushed my teeth, shaved, and put on the clothes I would have worn to work. She was still at the table when I came down. I was beginning to wonder if maybe she wasn't going to kill me. A nice thought, even if it would make the despair all that much worse when she finally did decide to kill me.

I said, "I'm glad you were able to come visit."

She got up. I squeezed my eyes shut, glad that at least I had already voided my bowels earlier and, on the off-chance that there was anything left of my corpse to identify, it wouldn't be wearing pee-soaked slacks.

She hugged me. She might have kissed me on the cheek, but I never saw which side of the bucket was touching my face.

I wondered, could a malak do nice things? Was it possible that God or whatever force was responsible for them might have made malaks do something other than murder us in the most undignified ways possible, desecrate our bodies and occasionally consume our remains?

I fumbled for the phone in my pocket. I called work and told them that I was very sorry, but I was going to have to use up all of my vacation, sick days, everything, which came to about a week. I mean, I couldn't go to work with a *malak* in tow, could I? I would have been fired.

Kim, my supervisor, said, "Can you at least give me a reason?"

I said, "I've got company, very special company."

She said, "Who?"

I said, "Inillustrable Girl."

My guest didn't seem to be paying attention, but she must have known I was talking about her. Like most malaks, she had made up the name herself. I'm not sure inillustrable is even a real word. I looked it up in the dictionary once, and it was there, but of course she could have put it there herself. The definition was "unable to be accurately portrayed in visual media or art," so it must have had something to do with the fact that she was a shape-changer. Anyway, it was a better name than most of them had.

Kim said, "Holy shit!"

I said, "I'd appreciate if you'd try to use more constructive language." I was afraid Inillustrable Girl would overhear.

She said, "How long has she been there?"

I said, "About half an hour."

She said, "Have you called the police? The National Guard? The President?"

I said, "I can't imagine what good it would do."

She said, "Just keep us posted then. We're rooting for you." And hung up.

THE ONLY FRIEND YOU EVER NEED

I tried to eat but she kept watching me and I couldn't handle it. I offered her food but she didn't react. I asked her if she wanted to play a game, and we ended up getting out the Candy Land set that I keep in my collection in case my little nieces came to visit. I stacked the deck so she would win. She seemed to enjoy it.

That reminded me that I would have to call my tabletop gaming group sooner or later. We were supposed to meet that night. Four of us guys, we'd met a few years ago at a very large support group for people with anxiety about malaks. If you've never been to one, you probably at least know what I'm talking about. One of the therapists suggested we four start meeting outside the group because we shared a common interest. We played mostly role-playing games having to do with vampires, because we thought vampires are a good analog for malaks and it helped us manage our fears. For example, you can't stop a vampire; if it wants to get you, it can fly or turn into mist or find some way. Like malaks. You never know what kind of powers a vampire will have without facing one, because there are so many conflicting mythologies. Like malaks. People think vampires are sexy but they're really not. Like malaks. We wrote pages of these. I could go on.

I called the guys while Inillustrable Girl was in the bathroom (not using it, just in it). I had to leave messages because it was the middle of the day and they were all at work. After that I laid on the couch and passed out.

I guess Phil hadn't checked his messages because he was the one who woke me up. I leaped off the sofa because I thought Inillustrable Girl was yelling at me, but she was only standing nearby holding the box for Parcheesi.

I said, "Please excuse me a moment," and ran up to my bedroom, opened the window and leaned out. I said, "Phil, what are you doing?"

He said, "Aren't we getting together tonight?"

I said, "No, something came up."

He said, "What?"

I said, "I can't tell you."

He said, "Can't you at least let me in?"

I couldn't, and told him so. If he saw Inillustrable Girl then I was sure he'd die immediately, either by her hand or from the heart attack it would trigger.

He said, "Why not?"

I said, "I'm not wearing any pants right now."

He said, "Put some on. Please. I need this session. I really, really need it. The monster killed a guy on my street this week. I'm freaking out. Please. I mean, who have you got in there that's so damn important?" His eyes widened.

I looked behind me and found her standing over my shoulder, board game in hand.

Phil started laughing. I mean really loud, forceful, hysterical sort of cackling.

I said, "Phil, get out of here."

He said, "There's nothing I'd love to do more." He had fallen over by this time, and had to choke his words out between sobs of laughter.

I said, "Then please go. Don't worry about me. I think I'll be okay."

He dismissed my assumption of concern using a very rude expression. Then he said, "She's gonna kill me, isn't she? She's waiting for me, isn't she?"

I said, "Phil, go. This isn't funny."

He said, "Please help. It hurts so much."

If I called the police, they'd want to come in and ask questions. Instead I called a cab. It was actually really easy to manage because Phil had passed out by the time it arrived. When I saw him lying there, I went out and checked his pulse, then put the cab fare in his pocket along with his address on a piece of scrap paper. I fainted myself shortly after, but Bob was gone when I woke up. Inillustrable Girl was not.

I suppose I felt a little surer of things by the second day, but I decided it would be best to call Siobhan and beg off dinner. She and I had started seeing each other a couple months ago after I

THE ONLY FRIEND YOU EVER NEED

pronounced her name correctly on the first try, and we had got to the point where we got together a few times a week. I thought that this, of all things, she would surely have to understand, but when I called her she insisted on coming over. Siobhan was terminally impulsive, which was less often beneficial than the romantic comedies would lead you to think.

There was nothing I could do to stop her from getting in. I tried to buttress the door with a bookcase, but I couldn't get it to actually lean against the door because of the way the floor bowed. She pushed the bookcase over without much trouble and came in.

She said, "That's her all right," referring to Inillustrable Girl, who was playing checkers against a bottle of Faygo which she had caused to become animate and invested with sufficient telekinetic ability to move the pieces. She was winning. "How long has she been here?"

I said, "It has been my absolute pleasure to have this wonderful guest for about two days now." Meanwhile I was moving the bookcase back where it belonged and putting the books back in alphabetical order by author. Siobhan could have helped me but she did not. She had always shown a certain irreverence for property. I reflected it was good that she had pushed over the bookcase instead of breaking a window to get in.

I continued, "By the way, I thought you wouldn't be able to make it."

Siobhan caught on to my implication, that I did not think it was safe for her to come over. She said, "What have I told you so many freakin' times that I'm sick of it?"

I said, "That there are certain things I would prefer not to mention right now."

She said, "By which you mean that if Inillustrable Girl is going to kill me then she's going to kill me, and if she's not then she's not."

Inillustrable Girl harkened curiously at the mention of her name. She then moved a gamepiece and exploded blue ribbons out of her bucket, which I had learned was her way of saying "king me."

After my blood unfroze I said hopefully, "Then we can go on seeing each other?"

She said, "Of course not."

I said, "That's fair."

I did not share Siobhan's philosophy, of course, and wanted to get her out of my house as soon as possible. I really did care about her, more than a guy like me is really good at giving words for, and I was nearly jumping for joy that she suddenly seemed to share my fear that she would be killed if she stayed.

But then she said, "I want to be clear that I'm not leaving because I'm afraid she's going to kill me."

I said, "You're not?" in a voice that I freely admit sounded much like a balloon deflating.

She said, "No, I'm leaving because I'm afraid she's going to kill you. I think she is. I know she is. I can feel it."

I said, "The way you could feel that the Challenger was going to blow up, even though you were a baby?"

She said, "Yes, exactly like that. I don't have these premonitions very often, Seth, but when I do they're accurate. And I can't bear to see that happen. I love you, Seth, I love you and so I have to leave you for fear of losing you."

I said, "I don't know what to say."

She said, "Goodbye, which is what I'm saying right now."

I said, "Goodbye," but she was already gone.

She had not said the, uh, what do they call it in movies, the L-word before that conversation. I wished she could have chosen another time to bring it out. Or just not done it at all. I had real trouble with relationships in those days. You remember when you were a kid, and you first realized that you were going to die someday, and for a while it made you kind of afraid to live because that would mean you were getting there faster? But you eventually got over having to think about it all the time, and just went about your business? I guess some of us people with malak issues never really got over that, never got over being afraid to love someone because with malaks you never know when you might open the door and see . . .

Sorry. Sorry. I still have trouble talking about this. Anyway it's not that important.

On day three I had what may have been a minor heart attack and started applying for jobs in other cities. One thing about malaks, I

THE ONLY FRIEND YOU EVER NEED

thought, is that they're violently territorial. They mostly have everything carved up so there's only one in each city or town, except for really big cities like New York, which has one for each borough. If I had an excuse to move, I would be able to get away from my guest. Probably.

I needed to look for new work anyway. If my week of vacation ran out and I didn't show up at work for three days straight, Kim would be required by company policy to fire me.

On day 4 my mother called. She said, "Honey, your father and I want you to know that we love you and we support your choice even if we don't agree with it."

I said, "What choice?"

She said, "We realize that not everybody loves the same way—"

I shouted, "I don't lllllllllll—!" It could have been a disaster. Trying to make up for myself, "I don't think you understand the nature of the situation."

She said, "But Siobhan told us all about it." She still pronounced it *soy-bun*. "You're living with the malak, aren't you?"

I checked my peripheral vision and contented myself that Inillustrable Girl was in the kitchen microwaving a can of tomato soup. I said, "It's the other way around, but yes, basically. It's not my choice and I'm trying to do something about it."

She said, "I understand, honey, but *hypothetically*, if it *was* your choice and you didn't want to tell anyone, we would support you too. But we're never coming to visit you again and you're never coming to visit us. Is that understood?"

I whispered, "I'm looking for a j-o-b on someone else's turf. Can either of you help me?"

She said, "Glad to hear it, honey. We love you." And hung up.

You know, the way people deserted me in those days, it was almost funny. Maybe now, after all the changes we've all been through, I could look for some of them, try to make amends, but it doesn't seem so important anymore.

Inillustrable Girl appeared at my side and brandished a bowl of hot tomato soup, splashing a bit on my chest.

I said, "Thank you so much. I was just thinking about lunch. However, I seem to have burned myself on the phone. Excuse me."

I was beginning to suspect that Inillustrable Girl was sticking around because she actually liked me. Weird to think of, isn't it? A malak liking someone. Really, feeling any way toward a person other than murderous or indifferent. I wasn't sure if it was possible. At the support group, they always talked about being able to view malaks as a metaphor. A personification of the unpredictability of death, I think was how they were always putting it. It's silly, I know: malaks aren't metaphors, they're real. The idea was that if we could come to terms with our own mortality then we could come to terms with malaks, though, so I had gotten used to at least trying to actually think of them that way, as a fixed idea that stood for one thing and nothing else. And now this.

It actually wasn't bad, for tomato soup. I mean, you know, the tomato soup wasn't.

I think what I'm trying to say is that my mom had brought up the question, even though naturally I couldn't feel *that way* about a malak, of whether maybe Inillustrable Girl felt *that way* about me. By day four she was doing what you might call cuddling, whenever I was sitting or lying down. She would em—embrace me, understand, and rest her bucket head on my shoulder. Day 5 saw her doing it even when I was standing up. Randomly. Just, whenever. I had to wonder whether she would eventually want to do *that*. I mean. Well, make love.

Okay, so night five. Um, I'm going to lay it straight here. Nothing to hide. She came up to my room and cuddled me for a while. Got up—to leave, I thought, but then she straddled my leg. My thigh. She never took her clothes off but I could, well, feel that she was, shall we say anatomically correct, you get me? I've never been very buff, so when she put her weight against. My thigh. There wasn't a lot of flesh between her and the bone. And she started. What's the word? Grinding. Just harshly rubbing herself back and forth. Basically masturbating with my femur. That's where the femur is, right, your thigh? She didn't make any noise, but I could still see that she was, um, experiencing—huh. I've never been good at this. There was some moisture.

Anyway that's the gist of it. It never went further than that. If it had, I wouldn't have any reason to pretend otherwise at this point, would I?

On day six I got a job interview.

THE ONLY FRIEND YOU EVER NEED

My mother actually had passed along my plea for help, as it turned out, to my father who knew someone from high school who ran a restaurant attached to a gas station in a place called Adams Township, not far from Zanesville. It had less than a thousand people, three churches and almost nothing else. I wasn't angry at dad. He'd tried. On the few occasions when he did come through for me, it was usually in this kind of way.

All the same, I didn't like the idea of working there. The local malak was supposed to be called Ultra Sasquatch, and resembled an anorexic Chewbacca. People got killed there just like anywhere else, and one in roughly seven hundred? I didn't like those odds. I didn't want to ask how the job had come to open up.

Of course, like any small town, Adams was cheap. I *could* buy a house there. Literally, just buy it for cash. So there was that.

The town was hard to find. Partially because when I left home, there was Inillustrable Girl in the back seat of the car.

I said, "Not that I'm not glad for the company, which I am, but are you sure you want to come along? I need to drive pretty far."

Nod.

What could I do? I started the car, figuring she'd probably teleport out when I left town. That, or kill me. I kept wanting to see if she was still there, but I was afraid to look into the back seat too often. I worked out a system: every time I wanted to check the back seat, instead of doing that, I made my peace with God.

Thinking it would be safe, I checked the rearview when I entered Muskingum. Should have been in someone else's territory by then, and like any malak she wouldn't cross borders, right? Wrong.

I said, "Muskingum," as if just muttering absentmindedly to myself. No reaction.

I got lost a few times on the way to Adams. I was distracted, naturally, because what did this mean? Were we going to get in trouble? If I lived, would this be a famous scientific discovery or something?

Nevermind. There's nothing scientific about malaks.

By the time we finally reached Adams, daylight was starting to wane. I apologized to my father's high school friend, a balding, emphysemic man wearing a Brett Favre Packers jersey. He wasn't insulted. He had so little business, he said, that it didn't really matter when I showed up.

Inillustrable Girl had stayed in the car, thankfully.

It wasn't much of a job interview. He asked me a number of questions, mostly about my religious and political leanings. Depending what answer I gave, he would either move on to the next question or tell a story. For example:

Him: "You go to church?"

Me: "Yes."

Him: "You libertarian?"

Me: "Yes."

Him: "Don't you believe a damn word of those Canadians and their healthcare system. It's not free, they pay absorbitant taxes for it, and it's the worst healthcare anywhere. I know a guy whose friend's dad lived in Canada . . . "

He repeated himself a lot. I tried to kowtow to him, but I left convinced that there had never really been a job on the table. He just needed someone to talk to. I get that sometimes. Actually, I get that kind of a lot. I suspect I'm not the only one. Maybe Inillustrable Girl was the same, in a way. Do malaks get lonely?

By then it was dark, and I was going back to my car, and I swear to gosh I thought it was Tommy Chong. I thought, what's Tommy Chong doing next to my car? And then I felt so embarrassed because of course it was Ultra Sasquatch, I mean it had to be because it was naked and covered with long brown hair, and I was probably about to die and that had been my last thought.

Ultra Sasquatch was very fast, which I saw when it grabbed me. It wasn't a teleporter but it did move its beam-like limbs much swifter than seemed possible for something so long. Like a double-jointed windmill. I had read some things about it before I came, and it was supposed to have a hobby of bisecting people. You know how you tear a piece of paper in half, then you put the halves on top of each other and tear the halves in half, and keep doing it until it doesn't seem worthwhile anymore? That.

So he had me by my one arm and my other leg and then—I don't know how else to say this, he sort of *popped*. Exploded, I

THE ONLY FRIEND YOU EVER NEED

guess, the way I had always imagined it when somebody told me about feeding Alkaseltzer to a bird, only much bigger and grosser. All at once I felt hot and moist, so my first coherent thought was *I'm covered with sweat*, then, *no, I'm covered with blood*.

So there you have it: malaks have blood. I know, I was there.

Inillustrable Girl cuddled me as soon as I got in the car. That was when I realized that I couldn't call the police, if Adams Twp. had police. Not with her there. Instead I had to write out the whole explanation on the back of my Mapquest directions and leave it in the parking lot under a chunk of concrete that I found coming off the curb. I tried to leave it near enough to most of the entrails for them to find easily.

I got lost on the way home.

I expected to start getting calls by the next morning. I had left my phone number on the explanation. Nobody called, so they must not have found it.

The same thing happened in Coshoctan two days later. I should back up.

I got another interview in Coshoctan. The job title was "computer guy," which should give you an idea of both the size of the company and its seriousness. I had applied thinking that it might get me saved. Now I wasn't so sure. I wouldn't have told you this then, but I actually wasn't sure I would take the job if it was offered. Coshoctan had a malak named Sniffer whose kill rate was a hair above average, and who liked to transmogrify people into person-size boogers. Bodies would go unidentified for weeks. Maybe the devil I knew was better.

Inillustrable Girl hadn't changed her appearance since the day she attached herself to me. She hadn't killed anyone either.

She came along again. We ran into Sniffer, and she toasted him. She melted his nostrils shut with her heat ray and he suffocated. You've read the story. I mean, reading about it doesn't really compare to watching a giant nose suffocate in person, rolling around on the pavement with no mouth to scream out of, but you know what happened.

Just like the rest of you, I wondered if a malak could be good.

M.SHAW

Maybe if they could form an attachment to someone, like a dog, they could be shown proper ways of behaving. Maybe they could even learn good from evil. Become citizens. You laugh, but we know *so little* about them.

People noticed, this time. It was during the day, right out in public. I didn't go to the interview, just got the heck out of town as fast as I could. A deputy stopped me on the way back to Zanesville. I told him that I understood he had been sent under the most noble pretenses of collecting information about what had just occurred in town, and recognized that he was only doing his job and I could be accused of obstructing justice for trying to prevent him. Also that, while I acknowledged all of these things, I had a malak sitting in my car and this could be a very precarious situation for him. He left me alone.

That was day eight. On day nine I got a call from the *Plain Dealer* asking for information. For an article.

He (the reporter) said, "Is it true that you have a malak living at your house?"

I said, "No comment."

He said, "Is it true you were there at the scene in Coshoctan yesterday, and that you drove away hurriedly afterwards?"

I said, "A lot of people drove away from there pretty quick."

He said, "Can I come to your house and ask you some more questions?"

I said, "You can stay the—" I'm just telling you what I said here. I was very serious. I said, "You can stay the h-e-double-hockey-stick away from my property."

As I mentioned before, I live in a townhouse, not a real house, and it's not actually my property. I rent.

He said, "When did you first meet the malak?"

It went on like that. If he ever showed up at my place it must have been while I was out of town, which happened a lot in the following days. When he finally hung up, I couldn't figure out who I had been trying to protect.

On day ten I realized that I loved Inillustrable Girl, following a conversation I had with myself in front of her, basically explaining some of the things I explained to you just now, about how she seemed to actually like me and maybe she was a good person at heart and all that. She cuddled me afterwards. It was kind of sweet. Well, maybe you had to be there to appreciate it.

THE ONLY FRIEND YOU EVER NEED

I know it's hard to bridge the gap between that and love, like capital-L love. If this adds a bit of clarity to the situation, it had to do with the fact that everyone else had left me and she hadn't, that she seemed to listen to me when nobody else did, that she was increasingly the most reliable thing I had ever had in my adult life and that, afraid as I was of her, she didn't seem to ask much of me.

Put it this way: a malak is the only friend you ever need. Not that, you know, you *can* have other friends with a malak around. But with Inillustrable Girl I had begun to understand that those other people? Never really had been my friends. They had never killed for me. They were there for me only some of the time. Their friendship was incomplete, not to mention conditional. That's the way it is with humans, even the most devoted human lovers. With a malak, friendship—love—is absolute. Maybe that's why it happens so seldom.

I still didn't dare cross her, though.

On day eleven I got a reluctantly-worded termination notice in the mail and realized that I was on a mission, possibly from God. I made plans. On day twelve the road trip started.

This is the part you're most familiar with already. The part they—remember, they—started calling the, uh, Great Malak Liberation. Hard for me to think of it that way anymore, even harder to say it. They meant, of course, that we were liberating people *from* malaks, not liberating malaks, which is kind of what it sounds like. But I don't have to tell you that.

Oh boy.

Okay, well here's the gist. Malaks blowing up, burning, falling over left and right. We went from town to town, mostly in Ohio, but going into West Virginia a little bit because we felt sorry for them. We went to Marietta and got Slap Man. We went to Parkersburg and got Smoking at Night. We went to Athens and got Look Ma No Hands. There were reporters. They took our pictures. It was the first time a malak ever posed for the press. The skull painted on her bucket seemed to be a little more smug than usual.

The said, "Who are you?"

I said, "We are Seth Miller and Inillustrable Girl, from Zanesville."

They said, "Why are you doing this?"

I said, "We're on a mission." I thought I remembered saying "from God," but they must have cut that out on television and in the papers. Maybe I didn't say it.

We went to Point Pleasant and got Tuxedo Piñata, who proved to be full of candy instead of entrails. We went to Huntington and got The Conjoined Collaborating Romance Authors. We went to Ashland, which was the only town we did in Kentucky, and got Ronald McMcMcShutUp. We went to Portsmouth and got Simply Beans. People started to turn out in droves when they heard we were coming. They would watch the fights, I guess because they were so confident in us.

They started to offer us things. We never had to buy gas or food, for one. But there were presents too, all kinds of gadgets and fancy bibles and valuable jewelry and people wanting me to marry their daughters, or even for Inillustrable Girl to marry their sons. In Portsmouth a car dealer showed up and offered us a brand new Mercedes, which I turned down.

I said, "I'm sure it *is* better than my Elantra, but isn't that kind of like offering Superman a new cape?"

And people *agreed*, my gosh, they agreed! See how out of hand it got?

By the time we got to Chillicothe they were actually throwing rose petals in the road in front of our car. Can you believe that? We were being followed around by a camera crew. It was supposed to be for a reality show that had been hurriedly arranged a couple days before. Naturally, that show never aired. Maybe you could find the footage somewhere if you were very dedicated. The mayor had the key to the city all ready to go, and after we turned Caramel Macchiato into a smear of moist espresso grounds against the side of the courthouse the whole town had a huge party. If they have an open container law there, they certainly were not enforcing it.

There was this, this *orgy*? Not planned, I don't think, definitely impromptu. I guess . . .

I felt bad about Siobhan.

I guess you never know about these people in these minor cities.

Siobhan though: I bet she would have been able to handle these things better than I did. She's more intense than I am. I mean, she

THE ONLY FRIEND YOU EVER NEED

has, like, more feelings. That sounds dumb. I'm not intense. When I was in school I got C's and D's in English. I read *Animal Farm* and thought Snowball was the villain. I'm not good at understanding things, is what I'm saying. People in larger-than-life situations who don't understand things usually don't last as long as I have. If Inillustrable Girl had interviewed people for this I would not have gotten the job.

So. Columbus. The, uh, day of destiny. As it were.

If you don't know, the malak there is named Comrade Cellulite, and she's a pregnant woman who is an octopus from the chest up and a humongous cow's udder from the waist down. You might have seen a picture, but it's hard to tell the exact composition because she has so many appendages, every one of which shoots acid, or occasionally LSD depending on what kind of mood she's in.

I swear, the way people turned out you would have thought it was Tyson vs. Holyfield. That was that big boxing match, right, Tyson and Holyfield? I don't really pay that much attention to boxing. Any, really, but. You know. They blocked off downtown. It even looked like Comrade Cellulite was in on it, because she was waiting for us on the statehouse lawn, in front of a statue of President McKinley.

I can't get the image out of my head. We got out of our car, me and this malak who I love. M—my Inillustrable Girl. In her ratty clothes, with her bucket head and her slouchy walk. She got out of the car, cracked her knuckles, and my God, she looked cute. I told her so, for the second time. I was confused, but the memory, I still treasure it a little bit.

The fight . . . did not go well.

I don't know why this possibility had not occurred to me before. I must have been too wrapped up in. Things.

She's not dead, I remember thinking right at the end. *She transformed into acid so that the blasts couldn't hurt her, and she escaped.* Which, frankly, was bull. Her body was right there in front of me.

That was a heck of a moment. Everybody standing around like, What happens now? All of us watching Comrade Cellulite sitting on top of the half-melted McKinley statue, wondering what she was going to do next, if we were all about to die.

M.SHAW

That reminds me, have you ever been to one of those support groups? You know what they tell you? They tell you that wondering if you're about to die when you see a malak is pointless. They tell you that we're all going to die, that while some of the causes may be different, people aren't dying any more or less often than they ever have, and when our time comes it will come and there is nothing we can do but accept it, and worrying about it is just an unnecessary source of stress.

They are so full of *shit*.

Comrade Cellulite stuffed herself back down into the sewers and we all thought we were safe.

―――✯―――

Hating malaks is a strange notion, isn't it? At least, that's what they tell us in the, you know, the focus groups. That it's like hating the weather, or cancer, or anything else you can't change. Everyone gets a little upset about these things now and then, but if you let it in and let it consume you . . . I mean, what would be the point? Hating them would make no difference, so nobody thinks of it. I had never hated malaks before, and I don't think anyone I knew had. They would say it off-hand, "I hate malaks," at funerals and things, or when they read about the rare celebrity death; but then, people say they hate snow or certain movies or their siblings all the time and they don't really mean it, it's just hyperbole, or not knowing what else to say.

I had this list though. I'd made it at the start of the road trip, when I was planning our route. I was crossing malaks' names off as we went along, *Kill Bill* style, only it was a much longer list. In the following days, before I finally tore up the list and flushed it down the toilet little bit by little bit, I kept looking at the spot where the crossed-off names ended (Comrade Cellulite was the last one, I'd crossed it out in pen before the fight, which sort of ticked me off afterwards) and starting to really hate the malaks who had dodged the bullet, if you will. Started to hate what they did, and the fact that they could just go on doing it as if they had never been in any danger. It took the real possibility of an alternative to make me feel that way. A lot of other people probably thought the same way, but I never learned of it then and now I don't think I ever will.

THE ONLY FRIEND YOU EVER NEED

I shacked up in the Hyatt a block away for—a long time. I stopped counting the days, and apparently so did the hotel because I never got a bill. I think there was some kind of *understanding* going on, if you get me, like I had become untouchable. My room never got cleaned even when I hung the little hanger with the picture of the wasp-waisted maid on it on the doorknob, so there you go.

I couldn't leave town. Couldn't bring myself to leave town, that is. I imagined it as being so sad, with the shot framed in my mind of my car receding into the distance, defeated, with the million people I had let down all watching.

I'm sure I must have eaten and changed clothes and all that, but I can't remember exactly how it worked.

The next solid spot in my memory is from what must have been weeks later, when one of the maids accidentally left a *Dispatch* in front of my door in the morning, even though I wasn't supposed to get the paper. The cover story: the entire area of Adams Township was a quarantine zone. Military blockades at every road into town and a perimeter set up around the area. They weren't releasing any information but a news chopper that had flown around just outside the no-fly zone reported that the town was just *gone*. Even the buildings. Nothing there. It was speculated that inside the area Ultra Sasquatch was alive and killing anyone who entered his territory. Sniffer was back in action too, in Coshoctan. The streets were littered with giant balls of snot, way ,way, way above his normal kill rate, or any other malak's, and the Governor had ordered the place evacuated. Washington had decided it was a pattern and FEMA was on its way in.

Come to think of it, maybe she didn't leave the paper there on accident.

They came back a day or so at a time, like clockwork, right in the order we had taken them out before. They evacuated all the towns, but then the malaks started showing up outside of their established turf. Tuxedo Piñata was the first one—I guess he particularly had reason to be indignant about things and was thirstier for revenge than the rest—but within a few days it was all of them. Then malaks who hadn't been killed started going crazy too, and when that happened all bets were off.

Now nobody is safe anywhere.

Safe, you get that? We were *safe* before, with the old malaks. Weird to think of, isn't it?

Some things which are all equally true: (1) I feel, in some way, responsible for what happened. (2) I could not have known that things would turn out this way. (3) I messed things up for everybody, regardless of where blame might lie. (4) If the balance was this fragile, it's a miracle we lasted this long.

At this point Inillustrable Girl had not yet surfaced. Comrade Cellulite had also gone MIA since the fight, so people were worried about that too, and given the way she came back later, rightly so.

Nobody ever tried to contact me, that I know of. Family, friends, co-workers, not even Siobhan. With Inillustrable Girl I had lost everything. I hadn't known this before, I mean really known what I had, what was at stake. I was stupid, I suppose, in that sense. I handled this thing poorly. A woman had reached out to me in love, and I had responded inappropriately. Which I've been accused of before.

Did I say a woman? I'm almost positive I said a malak.

Then one day, something happened that I had truly not expected: I went home. I got up early that morning. I went down to the gift shop in the lobby and bought some tooth paste, and brushed my teeth with my finger because I hadn't bought a toothbrush and hadn't thought of using the wash cloth. I ran a wet comb through my hair, which I saw had receded quite a bit, and looked for some Febreeze to spray my clothes but didn't find any.

At some point the hotel manager came to my door. "Son," he said, patting me on the shoulder, "it's time." I nodded, and he said again, "It's time."

I got my car out of the garage. Drove to Zanesville, my head empty all the way, feeling like I had spent the last few weeks sitting in a movie theater after the credits had finished rolling. That kind of total intellectual silence. On the highway, a few off-ramps were blocked with concrete barriers, spray-painted with the word "QUARANTINE" in orange. My exit was still open.

I came to my townhouse. In the front yard, Phil, arranged in glass mason jars sorted alphabetically by body part, so that the

THE ONLY FRIEND YOU EVER NEED

yard looked like a giant, putrid makeup kit. I only knew it was Phil because his clothes were nailed to the front door. Phil had all these *Star Wars* t-shirts with holes in the armpits that he never wanted to get rid of.

I wondered if finally being killed by a malak had set him at peace.

I still can't decide if this was supposed to be a present for me when I got there. Even knowing Inillustrable Girl as I do. There's still a lot of things about her I don't understand, like why she went on killing the other malaks as long as she did. She must have known what was up. Did she do it because she knew it was what I wanted? Because she thought it would teach me a lesson? I guess it could even be that she was unaware, herself, of what was really going on.

My keys had gotten lost along the way somewhere, so I dug the spare out of the flowerpot on the stoop and let myself in. The apartment was clean, the way I had left it, but everything was covered with dust so that it looked hazy, as if I were watching my place on an old TV set.

As soon as I came in, a bucket resting on the kitchen counter levitated and turned to look at me. Her face was an X made with rust. She had no body. She had removed any trace of humanity about her.

I thought I knew what was about to happen. I took a deep breath, made my peace. She floated toward me. I closed my eyes, but not tight. I could feel her near me. I knew I deserved what I was about to get.

I said, "I don't mind as long as it's you." *Maybe* I started to cry a little.

At a moment in which I felt I should not have still been alive I felt an invisible finger touch my face. That was this mark here, the one on my temple. When I finally opened my eyes, the way she looked at me—I mean, it was a rusty X on a bucket but it was *looking* at me, oh, you bet it was—I knew just was she was saying.

Oh, no. You're not done. We're not anywhere near done yet.

And then I died.

M.SHAW

When she put me back together, I told her that she had been right. We were not done. I said it because she had made me understand. Her, I mean. What it was like. Why we have to do what we do now.

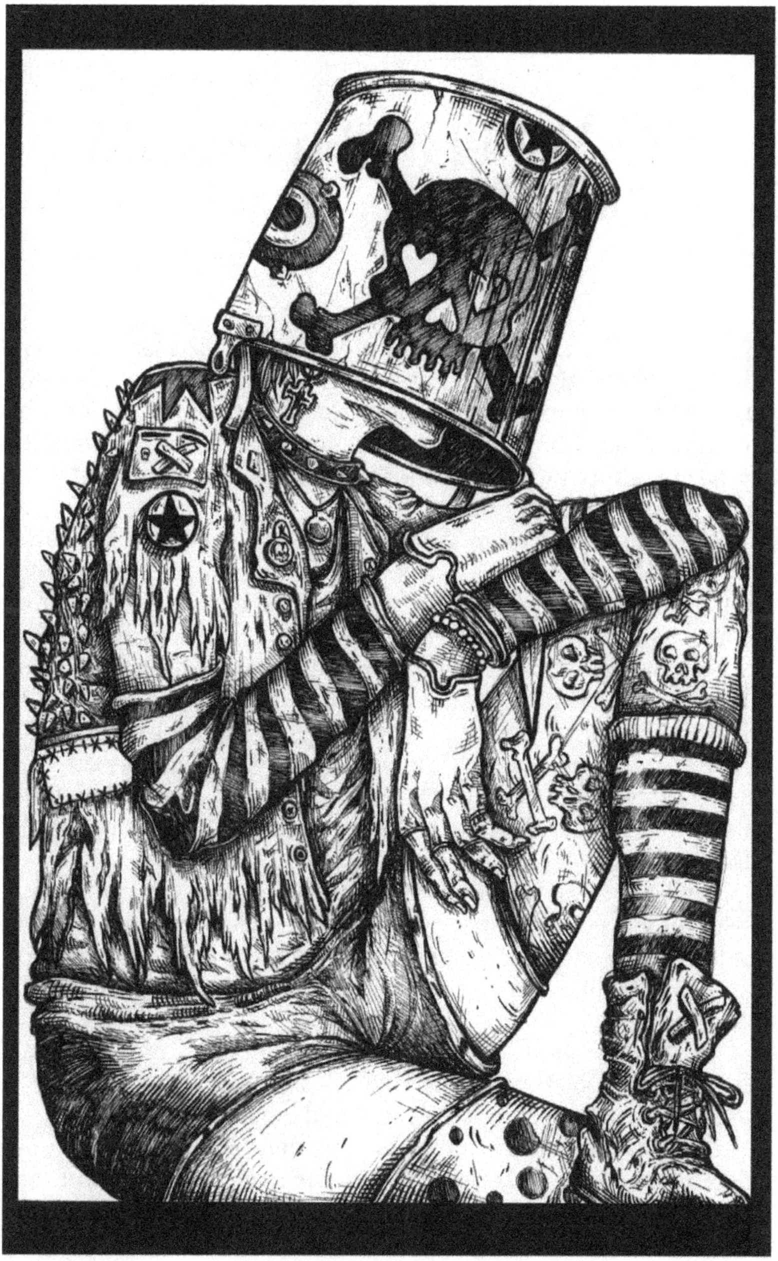

GO WITH THE FLOW

THE FIRST JOB post-surgery is a kitchen remodel. The handyman agency puts you on it along with a couple other guys, because you've worked with this customer before and apparently they liked what they got. You've lost an arm and had it replaced with a fancy, experimental bionic since then, though, so who knows if that opinion will hold up.

You walk in the door of the hideous suburban cookie-cutter monstrosity, the kind that was popular forty or fifty years ago when having money meant living far away from the city's center, rather than close to it. The woman of the house cocks an eyebrow when she sees you hauling in your tool bag with your flesh-and-blood left arm while the prosthetic right arm dangles unladen.

"Car accident," you say, raising the new limb for display. You figure it's best to get this out of the way, and firing off your explanation in such a short, one-liner fashion is much more palatable for everyone involved than talking about what actually happened.

"Oh," she says. Her tone of voice wavers more than you would have thought possible for a single syllable, like she's unsure what kind of emotion she's supposed to portray so she's just going to throw in little bits and pieces of all of them. For the follow-up she settles on, "Are you okay?"

"Better than ever." You give her a smile. "It's great for demo' jobs. We're taking the tile out, right? Won't know what hit it."

She responds with a deeply affected laugh.

The truth is that the bionic is considerably weaker than your original arm, and you are very, very far from "better than ever." Better than last week, maybe, but that's not saying much. Every time you think about the arm, which is often, you get this urge to

GO WITH THE FLOW

poke at the seam where it attaches to the stump on the end of your shoulder. There's this little line of blue plastic or rubber or something, just a tiny bit smaller in circumference than what's left of your bicep. It's hard to see, but impossible not to feel. Dr. Gleib, the lead surgeon, told you this part is called the *cuff gasket*, and that it's supposed to be a little tight to keep any "foreign matter" from getting "in there." What this specifically means is a mystery to you, but it sounds bad in a nebulous way. Everything about this device is ominous.

You set the tool bag on the kitchen counter that you're shortly going to start ripping out. With your left hand free, you immediately start digging at the little blue seam with one finger, as if to give your flesh some breathing room. It's only a little tight, like the doctor said; not painful, but it's *there*. It's not going away. This is your arm now.

Not for the first time, you wish you really had lost the original in a car crash, the way you tell people. The fantasy scenario is one where you're knocked unconscious and wake up in the hospital with the arm already gone, but you'd be willing to settle for a quick and dirty rip if you had to be awake for it, maybe a wedge of jagged metal cleaving off the limb before you realize what's happening. Losing an arm quickly must be awful, but it can't be as bad as losing it over a period of days.

Dr. Gleib told you the condition is called "acute compression syndrome." A heavy object—say, a cinderblock—can fall on you and cause a lot of pain, but not the kind you think is worth going to the hospital over, especially when you can still move the arm without much trouble. The next day it feels worse, but you might figure that's just the healing process at work, and if you go with the flow then it'll work itself out the way things always do. The day after that, it's much worse and you can't move it anymore, and it keeps getting worse from there.

When you finally do go to the ER, they'll explain to you that your arm has died. For three days you've been feeling it die, as swollen muscle tissue crushes the nerves and blood vessels inside. They'll tell you that your own body has been screaming at you for help and you've been ignoring it, and because you refused to listen, a piece of it has gone and decayed right off the whole living assembly. *How could you do this? How could you let this happen?* will be the thing they won't say, but it will be in the air all around you throughout your hospital stay.

When something like this happens to a guy, you can hardly be blamed for pretending it was a car crash. This way, no one else has to think about it or ask all the questions that pop into their head as a result, so that you have to relive the whole thing over and over as you explain it to them. This way, they'll just picture some scene from a movie they saw, and maybe even find it a bit exciting.

Even if the arm isn't strong enough to break up tile all by itself, the traditional hammer and pry bar thankfully still get the job done. The worry had been that you'd show up today and find yourself unable to do anything at all. One month after surgery you're supposed to be healed enough to return to work, but there's something uncomfortable about the interval; it feels like too short a time, even though living through it felt like an eternity of idleness. You guess any convalescence would seem too short on the first day back. Even if you waited a year or more, it would still feel like jumping in with both feet.

Besides, you can't afford not to work for more than a month. That was the deciding factor when the hospital offered you this whole "clinical trial" deal. Nobody said as much, but you knew it was either this or find a new career. You're not union, so no working arm means no handyman work, and fast food or retail won't pay the bills.

Anyway the thing's attached to you now, and even so, it's slow going. Maybe this has to do with the way the arm supposedly draws on your body's heat and metabolism for power, a mechanical vampire sucking away lifeblood.

Thankfully, none of what you're doing here today is all that fine-detailed or particularly strenuous. At some point in the not-too-distant you assume you're gonna have to hang drywall with this thing, and that's gonna be an adventure, but not today. Today it's the familiar, endless succession of hitting the old tile with a

GO WITH THE FLOW

hammer, scooping it up with the pry bar, and putting the pieces in a plastic drum. Fill up the drum, take it to the Dumpster, repeat.

At first you try breaking with your left hand and prying with the right, figuring that your non-dominant hand should be able to do something as simple as swing a hammer. But the muscles in your arm start tightening up quicker than you'd expect, and soon enough it's the robot hand holding the hammer and the pry bar alternately.

The new arm doesn't get sore, exactly, but there's something uncanny about the way it feels. The way the vibration travels up the hammer and into the arm. Each time you hit with the hammer, the weight of the arm pulls on your stump as it rumbles. To a certain extent, it's like the *tile* is hitting *you* with the hammer.

When you finish with the tile, a sense of relief spreads over you that is also a sense of extreme nervousness, and neither of these seems all that appropriate. It's just a bunch of ceramic fucking tile, it's a simple task, there's no reason to get weird about it. You lean on the wall and take a few deep breaths as the two other guys are moving the new dishwasher into place. One of them looks to you for help and you just shrug, seeing as how you're still not allowed to lift anything that heavy, even with straps.

The customer nudges you on the arm. The arm itself doesn't have nerve endings inside, so you don't feel the contact directly, just a jostle around the seam—the *cuff gasket*. You look at her. She's offering a beer, and you're fairly sure she's changed clothes for some reason.

"I can't drink on the job," you tell her, and suddenly you realize why you've felt so damn nervous this whole time. She's been watching you, not just the kitchen remodel in general but you specifically. Her eyes have been drilling into you from the living room all morning.

She taps the arm with the beer bottle, like the world's weirdest toast. "I already opened it. Come on, don't make me drink alone." You're not sure what to say, leastwise in front of the other guys. Eventually she picks up on this. "Suit yourself. I'll save it for you after work. Maybe it won't go flat if I stick it in the fridge. Can I ask a weird question?"

"Shoot."

She nods, glancing down at your new most interesting feature. "Do you have to lubricate it? Like, with oil?"

You answer "No," but your brain immediately goes *fuck, man, do I?* That does seem like a logical thing for a metal arm to need. Maybe the doctors neglected to tell you, assuming that one of the many other doctors you saw throughout the whole awful process would have told you already. You know what happens to a car if it doesn't get the oil changed regularly. What if the same is true of the arm? What if you're *already* supposed to have gotten the oil changed? Anyway, now you're thinking about car crashes again, and the twisted fantasy you have about lying in a pool of your own blood by the side of the highway, screaming in agony but blissfully unaware of what it feels like to be part corpse for three days.

"I just figured it must be something you need to stay on top of," she says. "I guess that's where my mind naturally goes. I'm pretty diligent about keeping things lubricated. And staying on top."

You feel the blood freezing in your veins (except in your right arm, which has none). This woman is a thousand percent married.

"Don't forget about that beer after work, okay?" She brushes her fingers against the arm before walking away.

All of the old appliances that you're replacing in this remodel are black enamel. All the new ones you're putting in are stainless steel.

Even before the customer brought up lubrication, making you preoccupied with maintenance in what was otherwise an attempt to make you preoccupied with pussy, you had recently found that you couldn't stop looking at the wrist. The way it rotates, specifically. You can see a little bit of it at the end of the forearm: there's some kind of ball-type-thing, although it's more oval shaped, and it moves around in its socket when you adjust the hand into different positions. Naturally the ball can't rotate all the way around, so only the part where it connects to the hand will ever be exposed to air. The rest will only ever see the inside of the arm.

That's the part that worries you. Everything looks fine now, but eventually the part that's exposed will need to be cleaned because it will accumulate dust and grime, plus it will probably get little scratches and other wear and tear, which will make it even harder to clean. None of the doctors said anything about this, but you see it all the time with stuff in houses. You take all the books off a

GO WITH THE FLOW

bookshelf and the wood underneath will be a different shade because it hasn't had all the light and air and dust hitting it for all those years. It doesn't matter how much you clean it or polish it, there will always be that visible difference, like a tanline.

Slowly but surely, the elements will take their toll on the exposed part of the ball. It'll get all pitted and ratty. It'll look like Swiss cheese. You haven't yet run into what to do when it needs major repairs. Haven't even asked Dr. Gleib or anyone else about it. That has to be a thing that they do, right? Whoever *they* are? They wouldn't just be attaching these arms to people's bodies if there weren't some kind of plan for how to handle things when something goes wrong, right? Because something always goes wrong. That's a fact. That's how the universe works. They thought of that, right? They must have?

But then again, what if they—the company that makes the arm, probably, or whoever it is that's responsible for this—what if they go out of business? Happens all the time. Commerce isn't exempt from *something always goes wrong*. Or maybe they wouldn't go out of business, but would decide prosthetic arms aren't profitable enough and they're going to shut down that wing of the business and for everyone who already has the arms, it's just like, good luck? That's what happened with your mp3 player back in the day; why would this be any different?

The real mindfuck about the whole thing is that, for the first time since you were a little kid, you have no concrete idea where your body came from. Not all of it. How do you even ask about something like that? Would Dr. Gleib sit you down and say, "Well, sometimes when a surgeon and a medical device manufacturer love each other very much . . . "

And now you're thinking about sex again. Caught in a fucking loop. Never gonna stop.

You spend the last three hours of the day thinking about how you'll convince the other guys to leave without you, and in the end what you come up with is, "I gotta stick around to take care of some things." Obviously your heart's not really in it. You're just going with the flow, per usual.

"What things?" says the older one, the guy who should probably be retired at his age but can't afford to; a preview of what's to come, for you, if you're lucky.

"I dunno, just some bullshit," you say. "I did the bathroom for this same house a while back, I think she's having some issue with part of that."

"You want a second pair of eyes one it?" says the younger guy, always eager to do more work as if it'll get him something, an uncomfortable mirror for your own younger self. "You gimme a ride home, I can stick around for a bit."

"Nah, I got this. It's not billable hours anyway." You've at least got a couple things working in your favor here: one, that you drove your own car to work, and two, that the other handymen are willing to take no for an answer. The older guy has been clicking his tongue all day whenever he sees the way the customer interacts with you, but if he knows what's up then he's too damn tired to say anything.

There is a moment, as you stand in the driveway watching them go, when you're acutely aware that you still have the chance to back out of this. Which, why wouldn't you? Best case scenario, if you go through with it, is that things are going to be incredibly awkward when you show up tomorrow to finish the remodel. You could just drive away now and she'd probably never bring it up again.

But isn't it easier to be swept along with the current?

You drink the beer (flat) and chat with the customer about the weather (hot). Apparently this is her version of foreplay, because she's leading you upstairs by the hand barely a second after you've finished your drink. You still aren't sure of this woman's name. It's on the work order for the kitchen job, but you always skim over that part of the form because all you personally need to know is the address where you're going and what you're supposed to do there. The most you can remember is that her last name starts with a P. Also you're pretty sure that her first name is either Krista or Lauren, though you can't figure why those would be the two choices.

"You know what this is, right?" she says, as she's shutting the bedroom door.

You assume *this* refers to whatever the hell is going on right now, so you say, "Yeah."

GO WITH THE FLOW

"Good," she says. "So take that big, metal arm of yours and rip my clothes off with it."

The real problem with this arm, you think, is that people look at it and think of the robot from *The Terminator* and get all these ideas about all the thrilling violence you must be capable of. What you need to do is get it painted gold so they'll think of the robot from *Star Wars* instead, the only character in the whole series who never fights anyone. That would be a much better match for how it feels to use the thing.

"Want some help with that?" she stage whispers as your fumble over her bra clasp like a fucking virgin.

You're struggling to ignore the fact that you just worked a full day, you're not as young as you used to be, and your body is a column of ache, especially your shoulder stump. Half the time it feels swollen, so that the goddamn *cuff gasket* is squeezing it within an inch of its remaining life, while other times it feels shriveled and hollow, rattling around like a coin in a tin where it's seated in the bionic.

"The fingers aren't really good for stuff this delicate," you explain. "At least, not if I can't see what I'm doing." You notice yourself whispering now as well. You're both behaving like actors who have forgotten their lines.

"You want me to turn around?" she whispers, turning around.

Your control of the last two fingers on the hand has been coming and going this afternoon, and the pendulum is currently swinging toward *going*. Left to their own devices they crook halfway closed, making it hard to do things like unhook a bra because the fingers push your hand farther away from her back. You need to periodically reach over and uncurl them. You wonder about maybe rigging some kind of system with rubber bands and, like, a pencil or something to keep them straight. Barely a month of using this thing and you're already having to work around its kinks, as if it were an old work truck.

The moment you finally get the bra off, she twists back around and moves the hand to her tit. "Ope." She chuckles. "It's cold."

"Yeah," you say, thinking, *I am about to have sex with someone who says "ope."* As your brain gets used to this fact, she puts her mouth on yours. It's amazing how you can just let things happen. You can reciprocate the kiss without really trying, without

M. SHAW

anything recognizable as thought or care, allowing yourself to exist as something like a video game controller; she presses the button and you do the thing. Maybe she even realizes what's happening. If so, great! This woman has clearly got some kind of thing for robots, and in this moment, that's what you are. One big, artificial limb. An entire prosthetic person.

And so everything proceeds as programmed. She's fully topless, so it's time for her to go down on you. She even unbuckles your belt herself while you stand there, arms dangling. You feel like there should be music playing.

You do your best to let go of all the stupid thoughts climbing the walls of your skull and enjoy the moment. You remind yourself that being in this situation would be a dream come true for a lot of people (shit, is *that* why the younger guy wanted to stick around?). It's basically the setup to a porn flick. A *bad* porn flick, which makes it all the more appealing, right?

Despite this, you're having a hard time maintaining arousal. Time to bring out the big guns: mentally scrolling through all the super weird shit in the porn folder on your computer, the one labeled "tax docs" that you've never so much as hinted at the existence of to another living soul. It's not like there's anything illegal in there, just a series of conversations you'd rather not have. Like, if someone saw it who you were dating then shit would get weird, even though these aren't things you actually want to do, just things it turns you on to look at, which would be so uncomfortable to explain that you've actively avoided thinking about it for your entire adult life. Or, if some friend of yours or a guy from work saw it . . . well, forget about it. You'll never give them that ammunition.

This still isn't working.

"Sorry," you say, "I need, uh . . . " You trail off, hoping someone (God?) will finish the sentence, since you don't know how to end it yourself. No dice. "It feels really good," you promise.

"Let's move to the bed," she says. "No fair you're the only one feeling good."

You seat yourself with your back against the headboard, pants down to your ankles because it seems counter-intuitive to be putting things back on at this point but you can't get the hems past your work boots. She pushes your knees apart, rests her back against your chest and guides the metal hand down the front of her

GO WITH THE FLOW

pants. This is good; it's something you can do without thinking, or, more accurately, while thinking too much. Obviously it *has* to be cold as hell.

Her sex sounds are purely nonverbal, amorphous moans and sighs that could be organic or manufactured. Either way you're getting the sense that this is really what she wants. Being finger-blasted by a cyborg. Not exactly your personal fantasy, but given the contents of your porn folder, who are you to judge?

Eventually you switch places, her getting fully nude and positioning herself under you so it's easier to crook your elbow and move your hand in a more vigorous, piston-like fashion. It's hard to tell how much pressure you're exerting, but she isn't complaining. You're at least fairly sure you've found the raised mass of folds that comprise the G-spot. The sensation is all different, fingering someone with a prosthetic. Except for the creeping soreness in your shoulder and half-bicep. All that time with the nail gun and table saw earlier. Replacing kitchen tile with hardwood is such an odd choice. Won't it be harder to clean? What was wrong with the tile? It looked almost new.

Speaking of cleaning, you're starting to wonder if this is good for the arm. What with the, you know, wetness. Dr. Gleib said it was fine to take in the shower, but are bodily fluids a different story? Maybe so. Maybe she didn't bring it up because it's never come up before. That would make sense unless some scientist or some other test patient has a partner who's keen on having a robot arm inside them. It's possible you're about to make some horrible new discovery about the corrosive properties of pussy juice.

Still, you do have to admit that this experience is kind of gratifying, from a certain angle. You're sure her sounds are genuine at this point, and the novelty of the whole thing does have its appeal. You're even starting to get aroused again, although the soreness in your bicep is getting extreme. When you glance at it, the flesh looks like it's being strangled by the prosthetic, veins throbbing as your heart desperately tries to pump enough blood into the appendage to give it the oxygen it needs (or thinks it needs, because your heart is a dumbass and still thinks there's a whole, real arm there). When you look away, it feels wobbly. Alarmingly so.

Don't think about this. Stop thinking about it. You're finally starting to get juiced up again, don't ruin it by focusing on the arm. Focus on the vagina.

You hear the front door shut. So much for getting juiced. "Shit."

"Don't stop," she whispers.

You remember meeting this woman's husband once before, during the bathroom job, and he is not in any way an intimidating man. If you remember right, he's some kind of computer guy, but hell, you live in a country with more guns than people, so who knows.

You try to pull the arm away and run for cover, maybe the closet, which you also installed on a previous job (these people are addicted to remodeling) and now wish you'd had to foresight to include a secret back-panel. But she grabs the arm by the wrist and won't let you go.

"I gotta hide," you whisper.

"I'm so close," she says. "Don't you dare stop, I'm so fucking close." It's unclear whether she heard you, which means she probably didn't hear the door either.

"I'm serious. I think your husband's home," you say, your whisper turning into a faint squeal for fear of volume.

Her legs clasp shut around the arm. You grunt loudly in response, because it feels like you're having a tooth pulled, the way she's wrenching it around with every ecstatic movement. This is godawful fucking embarrassing. The guy must know you're here now, because his wife is practically screaming while trying to pry the arm off with her cooch. You can't hear anything from downstairs, though. Maybe he's listening quietly, maybe he's screaming threats of murder that are being drowned out by the pounding inside your skull. You swear you can feel her sex moans vibrating in your bones, especially the titanium ones. It's a fucking earthquake in there. Even without nerve endings, you can feel that she's cumming on your hand, clenching down on the two fingers like a mousetrap.

As her orgasm crests, everything below the waist jack-knifes sideways. There's a sound that is somehow both a *crunch* and a *squish*, and suddenly the idea that she's trying to pry the arm off is more than a figure of speech. Through the intense and immediate pain, which is now far worse than having a tooth pulled, you can feel lengths of tubing being pulled taught, fuses snapping where

GO WITH THE FLOW

they attach to major blood vessels, a sort of *pop pop pop* like corn kernels in hot oil.

There's blood. Holy fuck, is there ever blood.

You can't tell where your scream ends and hers begins.

You're on the floor without any memory of the process of getting there. The husband has entered the room, and now he's standing on one side of you, saying something, and she's on the other side of you, saying something else. You can't make out the words, or their emotional tenor. Is he shouting accusations? Is this his fetish too, and he's starting his own chorus of orgasmic delight?

You can't stop laughing long enough to find out because, oh my god, this is *so bad,* this is so comically fucking bad. Once again, going with the flow has swept you clear out to sea, which is exactly what got you this evil fucking arm in the first place, so sure that you could simply ignore the pain and awkwardness and everything would work itself out somehow. And for better or worse, it did work itself out, just like it's doing now.

Goodbye, job. It was mostly tolerable knowing you. Goodbye dignity, if there's anything left of you hanging around.

With the arm gone, your shoulder feels lighter than air. The shoulder itself is burning up, or maybe the rest of you is getting cold, faint from blood loss, veins frozen and spasming in panic at the same time. The real shit part is that this is how you wish the original dismemberment had gone: a quick and dirty rip. Not a car crash, but close enough. You might not even bother to make up a story for Dr. Gleib, when she questions you about what happened. You can say *it was torn off in a freak cuckolding accident* and maybe she'll believe you or maybe she won't, but either way, what's she going to do about it? The arm's gone regardless.

And hey, look at that! There's a bright side to everything, huh. Silver linings. That hideous foreign limb is not longer attached to your body, and this time it had the grace to go the way you'd have preferred in the first place. You are finally lying a pool of your own blood and you are cracking the fuck up.

AS I WAIT FOR
THE KILLING BLOW

MY FIRST FEATHERS came in just a few days after my granddaughter Sima was born. Black as a raven's, but that doesn't mean much in the beginning. I could end up black all over, or a stormy grey color, or violet with blue speckles, for all I knew. The turning never brings the exact same form twice, just as no two children need the exact same monster to help them come into adulthood.

To no one's surprise, it was my son-in-law who had tears in his eyes when he saw them. Yermiyahu was his parents' fifth child and never had to slay an Ancestor. His four elder siblings had taken care of them all. One by one, the children were born; one by one, their grandparents grew horns, or scales, or wings, and fled into the hillside; and one by one, the children went to hunt them down when they came of age. Until Yermiyahu. Fifth children are sometimes called pine daughters (among less favorable names) because pine is a soft wood from a tree that grows up without ever having to drop its leaves. And he was no exception, fine son-in-law though he was.

"Come on, Yeyeh," I said to him at his daughter's naming ceremony, when he still couldn't look at me without his lip quivering. "This is supposed to be a happy occasion! We knew one of us would turn, and now you can look forward to the strong climber she'll have to become to face a flying Ancestor. I'm proud of her already. There's no reason to pity me."

"It's not you I'm scared for, mom," he whispered. "It's Sima. What if she can't . . . You know. Can't do it?"

"Can't slay me?" I allowed myself the smallest chuckle. "It's not fatherly to be so afraid for your daughter's failure, Yeyeh. You can't

AS I WAIT FOR THE KILLING BLOW

protect her from the dangers of the world. Not even when they look like her grandma." I extended my arm outward — no feathers there yet, but we both gazed up, toward my fingertips, imagining the powerful wing it would soon become.

"Promise me," he said. "When she comes of age, you won't fight her. Let her take you. Please, mom. I can't stand to think of losing her."

When my daughter, Rivkah, was five, just going to her first fencing lessons, the realization came to her that I myself might become an Ancestor one day. Every parent dreads this conversation, no matter how many books we read to prepare us. I could never forget the look in her eyes, the sound of her voice, when I answered her questions and tried to reassure her that it would not happen for a long, long time.

This talk with Yermiyahu brought those sensations back into focus, as if he were my five-year-old daughter instead of my grown child's husband. And so I talked to him as I had talked to her, back then. "I can make you all the promises in the world," I said. "And they will be the promises of an old woman. Whether the monster will hold herself to them is not for me to say."

"But it's still you," he insisted.

I nodded, though I couldn't stop my gaze drifting away from Yermiyahu and out the window to my right. "Yes, but only in the same way that I am still the seventeen-year-old girl who slew my grandmother. Now, I am on the other side of the equation. Time and age shift one's perspective in ways one can never anticipate. Parenthood involves a great deal of such reversals. You'll get used to it. This is just the final reversal for me." I placed my hand on his cheek, covered in bristly beard but still smooth underneath. "I'm not afraid for myself or little Sima. It's you I'm worried about, Yeyeh. Are you sure you're ready for all this?"

He sighed. "I thought I was, but I'm not so sure, these days."

"It was a rhetorical question." I smiled. "You don't have a choice in the matter anymore."

A deep breath. "You're right, of course," he said. He wiped his eyes, straightened the lapels on his jacket. "This is supposed to be a happy occasion. Do I look composed?"

"Hardly," I said, "but thankfully all your friends are here for your daughter, not you."

He nodded and returned to Rivkah's side.

M. SHAW

I let my eyes return fully to the window, imagining that I could feel another pair of eyes, great orbs of midnight, each one as big as my entire frail old body, watching back. "I'm coming soon," I whispered, then went to take in as much of my infant granddaughter's smile as I could.

The most irritating thing about turning is that there's no one to talk to who understands how much it hurts to feel your own bones hollowing themselves out for flight. As my full plumage comes in (tawny and sleek, like a kestrel), the floor of my home becomes littered with the little fuzzy pin feathers that preceded them. As if I were a newborn chick. I don't bother cleaning them up.

Sometimes they throw a celebration for the grandparent, but I wouldn't have it. They feel too much like a funeral, with polite relatives pecking at casserole and bobke, and music that alternates between nostalgic and somber. I don't feel either of those things. I'd be more suited to battle hymns, soaring requiems, screaming arias. The younger folks wouldn't get it.

The women in my family have always seemed oddly eager to turn, when the time comes. My parents used to tell me that, on the very day I was born, my grandma had sprouted big tufts of fur from her ears. Within a month, she had run into the hills on all fours, covered in a slick brown pelt. What she did for the next seventeen years is her business. I only know that she was still waiting when I came up there after her with a new shield and an old boar spear over my shoulder.

She was no more prepared to go down peacefully than I imagine I'll be. She had claws like spades and could fit her whole great, hulking body into the tunnels she dug with them. The first time she went underground, I made the mistake of climbing a tree to see where she emerged. Before I knew it, the ground I watched was rushing toward me as the tree fell into the tunnel she had dug beneath it.

I was fortunate not to break a leg in the fall and smart enough to make her chase me upslope, where the ground was all rock. Those claws weren't much good against boulders and cliffs. Then, she had nowhere to hide.

Rivkah was my only child. When she was born, it was my

AS I WAIT FOR THE KILLING BLOW

mother whose skin turned to scales, whose teeth and neck grew long before she skittered eastward, toward the desert. If anything, she turned even quicker than the stories I'd heard of my grandma. Rivkah never would talk about what happened out there, the week after her seventeenth birthday. I only ever knew that she came back with one less arm but nonetheless walking with her posture a bit higher — ready, at last, to learn a civilized trade.

It takes children and outsiders some time to understand that we aren't sad when our elders become Ancestors. We are not losing them, the way it happens with a disease or an accident or a war. When it happens, our fates are intertwined. It ensures that our moment of parting will be personal, that it will be self-determined, and that it renders the child an adult, if they survive.

I lost my husband to a kick from a draft horse. I'd rather have watched him grow these feathers and sent him off into the sky with a kiss on the beak.

My house has been empty ever since, mostly. Rivkah comes by every week to help me keep the place clean. On rare occasions, I do entertain another guest, but she only visits at night and never comes into the house. I watch the trees through my window, after sunset, not for a shape so much as an absence among them. A conspicuous darkness, sometimes punctuated by the glimmer of an eye in the moonlight. My guest doesn't talk much, and all I ever say are my little taunts. "I bet you'd like me to let you in, wouldn't you?" Or, "A little longer. Wait just a little longer."

Each morning, now, I get up and count the feathers that came in during the night. I take heart, knowing that I will not waste away. In my old age, I will grow strong again. And when little Sima comes for me, on the cusp of her adulthood, I know we will reach an understanding.

When Rivkah visits, now that she's recovered enough, she finds me in my place by the window, facing the hills, waiting for the day I will disappear skyward. We talk about Sima, clean the kitchen, make the bed. When she leaves, she hugs me a long time and says, "Goodbye, mother," as if it is the last time, because you never know. I've already grown enough that her arms no longer reach around my torso.

I tell her I love her, and that I'm proud, and all the things I've been promising to tell her in this moment, since she was small. But even she does not know what is in my thoughts. How could she? I never told her my whole story.

For I spared my grandmother, all those years ago. Upon the rocky hillside, I looked into her eyes as she waited for the killing blow, and I saw that this was not the path for me. Somehow, behind that inhuman visage, I recognized the details of the portraits I had been shown, the letters I had been allowed to read from before she changed. I couldn't say just what it was that I saw, except that it was a resemblance much deeper than a nose or a brow line or any of the other similarities between parents and their children that we often remark upon. Our people's poems and stories are full of such sentiments, but I never imagined that the familiarity would be so complete, so exacting and inexplicable at once. When I felt that, I knew that killing her would not make me understand what it is to grow up. There was a great journey between the woman who wrote those letters and the one who lay prostrate before me then, one that was invisible to me despite all I had been taught. She had more to teach me yet. She still does.

What I told Yermiyahu was not entirely true. I am still that seventeen-year-old girl. And I always keep my promises.

We don't really know what happens to the Ancestors who survive the coming-of-age rite. She is out there still, somewhere. Soon the turning will reach my feet, and make them talons; my arms, and make them wings; my heart, and make it hungry. I will fly back to the place in the hills I remember. I will find my grandmother. I will look into her eyes again. And I will finally give her what she has been waiting for, all this time.

Then, it will be my turn to wait. On the day Sima comes for me, I will look in her eyes as well, and we will reach an understanding of our own. I don't know yet what it will be, but I know that I will be so, so proud, and my talons so, so ready.

MY DAD BOUGHT A SPACE SHUTTLE

HE HAS TO park his truck in the street because the shuttle takes up the whole driveway. It sits there 360 days a year, with a giant tarp over it in the summer so the thermal tiles don't cook our house with reflected heat. The other 5 days a year my dad gets up early to hitch it to his truck and wake the whole neighborhood with his cursing while he hits the blocks from under the wheels with a sledgehammer. He drives it to a launch pad in the outer suburbs that used to be a soybean field, grumbling the whole way about traffic and how they'd better not give his time slot away just because he's a few minutes later than his reservation again. Usually one of his friends gets there ahead of him to hold the time slot, because they know how he is. He always blames my little brother Tony for making him late, which I think Tony considers the price of admission to space. He's been even more sheepish around dad than he used to be, ever since I got banned from the shuttle.

―――✈―――

I only got to go up the first two trips. My dad caught me smoking weed in the shuttle on Halloween two years ago with Aubrey, the lesbian from theater club who pretends to be my girlfriend for both our benefit. That's when the ban happened. "You're grounded," he told me, "literally grounded. You won't be going to space today, or this year, or until you graduate if I've got any say in it. Little shit. You won't be taking my shuttle for granted again." He convinced himself that Aubrey also had sex with me in the shuttle, which is why I also got grounded in the traditional sense for a week. I didn't bother to correct him. Every time he goes up I get a bunch of texts about how his friends say they can still smell the weed. I'm pretty sure it's just their farts, which are raunchy as hell and don't tend to dissipate when they happen in an airtight metal tube in space.

My dad takes his friends up into low orbit to drink beer and talk about how much it cost to launch the shuttle. He resents every dollar he spends, so one of the best ways to be friends with him is to talk about how much things cost, and the people who stick around in his life tend to be the same way. I mean, they talk about other stuff too, but that's always the first item on the agenda. They talk about the beer they're drinking; how they can never get the schedule they want at work; what kinds of smart devices they have bought, or are buying; how much they still owe on the loans for their shuttles; whether they can hold their poop until they get back to Earth, or have to cram themselves into the space toilet. The shuttle gets satellite TV. They went up there to watch the Super Bowl and the picture was *crystal clear*, as if they were right there at the game (in Kansas City).

My dad says it's great that ordinary people can take trips to space now. It used to be only a few people got to do it, and they had to go through all kinds of training. Not to mention, the government decided who could go, and the government deciding anything is a big red flag, in his book. Then along came the Lex Luthors, which is what I call the guys who invented commercial space flight, because their names all sound like "Lex Luthor" and it's easier than trying to remember which one's which. Now anyone can go, as long as they can qualify for a $750-K loan, plus the maintenance and launch costs. As great as he says it is, though, my dad doesn't seem any better off over it. He goes up there, uses the place as a home theater where he can float to the beer cooler, then comes back and gets mad at his cable news and goes to bed the same as always. He still hates his job, and my mom, and Tony's mom, and our

MY DAD BOUGHT A SPACE SHUTTLE

neighbors, and the weather, and whatever else the news tells him to hate. Sure, he's got bragging rights over people without space shuttles in their driveways, but so what? He used to have a speedboat in the driveway, and that was the same deal.

After I got banned from the shuttle, I got a job at Burger King. My dad thinks I'm saving to buy my own shuttle, since I'm not allowed in his. You'd almost think he doesn't know how much a shuttle costs, as if he didn't complain about that exact thing every chance he gets. I can afford other things with my paycheck, though. Makeup. Hair accessories. The odd piece of gender-affirming jewelry. No clothing yet, though; too much harder to hide that, or convince him it's a gift for Aubrey. But I *am* saving, so, eventually. In the meantime, I just have to deal with him telling everyone that I'm trying to buy a shuttle so I can have space sex with my girlfriend, but that it won't work because he won't let me park my shuttle on his property. It's supposed to embarrass me when he does this, but really I have to work hard not to laugh.

The shuttle has "Janice," which was my grandma's name, painted on the side. Tony and I just call it the Man Cave, which has a lot more to do with the shuttle than my grandma ever would have. My dad does have an actual man cave in the garage, but he never uses it anymore now that the shuttle has taken its place. I'm not allowed in there either, but whenever my dad is up in space I jimmy the lock so I can shut myself in and watch movies by myself. *Rent, Hedwig, Priscilla: Queen of the Desert,* all that stuff you'll get made fun of if people find out you like it. The garage is soundproofed, so Tony can't hear. I always get Aubrey to burn DVDs for me, so the movies won't show up in the streaming history.

M.SHAW

The shuttle's guidance software requires a monthly subscription. My dad says it's a scam, but he keeps paying for it anyway. What he doesn't pay for is the premium, ad-free version, which he says is an even bigger scam. Every launch and return flight, they have to sit and listen to a bunch of ads in a loop on the speaker. Basically, what plays in movie theaters before the previews. If you don't buy a subscription, the system locks you out and you have to chart everything manually, which means there's no knowing where you'll end up. Some rich frat bros from MIT tried it last year and they went down over North Korea and got shot out of the sky. The ones who survived the crash, the government had to negotiate for their release. One of them said in an interview that he doesn't regret doing it. I guess when you've got that much money, you don't have to regret much of anything.

When the Lex Luthors first talked about commercial space flight, they talked about terraforming Mars. They talked about opening up space for everyone. Then they got themselves up there, and started mass-producing the shuttles, and gradually they stopped talking about that stuff. We don't have colonies on Mars, we just have a bunch of people like my dad paying a grand a month to watch car commercials in zero-G. He still worships the Lex Luthors, though. Sometimes, while he watches the news, he'll name search them on social media to find people criticizing them so he can go off in the replies. I think it makes him feel like he's paying his dues.

The school guidance counselor says I should try to have empathy for my dad. He went through 2 divorces and he's been taking care of us mostly by himself for almost a decade. My mom and Tony's mom don't want anything to do with him. They didn't even want alimony or child support, because they already learned what happens when you accept anything he gives you. They've got visitation rights but they know better than to come around, so we only get to see our moms when we visit our grandparents.

MY DAD BOUGHT A SPACE SHUTTLE

Somehow, in this equation, my dad is the one who needs the empathy (according to the guidance counselor), and also the space shuttle (according to my dad). I go to a charter school, so the guidance counselor isn't a real therapist, he's a friend of the principal with a master's in film.

I think my dad is looking for an excuse to ban Tony from the shuttle too, so he'll be able to bring another one of his friends to space without going over the weight limit. I'm basically adult size but kicking me out didn't do any good, since all his friends are other truck drivers from his work with big beer guts who wear their steel-toes all the time because they think it's more manly. Tony's only 11, but that 105 pounds could make all the difference. So my dad's always chewing him out over every stupid thing. Problem is, unlike me, Tony's a figurative and literal boy scout. He always makes honor roll. He doesn't even play video games. What makes it even harder to watch is that Tony thinks dad's on his case because he's not a good enough kid. If dad tears him a new one because he was too busy doing homework to take the trash out before bed, he'll think it's his fault for not doing it faster. I've tried to help him get wise, but why should he listen to me? I'm banned from the space shuttle.

The Lex Luthors are too old to go into space themselves anymore. Nowadays, their thing is The Matrix. As in, the movie. They want to be able to cryogenically freeze their bodies and hook themselves up to a computer simulation of the real world. Well, the real world plus them being able to fly and whatnot. One of them keeps posting about having sex with VR catgirls in his Matrix. *All* of them post about living forever. They say their simulations will include time dilation technology to make a second out here last a year in there. None of this is even close to existing yet, but they've got all the money and people in the world, so who knows?

M.SHAW

Last November, my dad decorated the space shuttle with Christmas lights and an inflatable Santa, which he tethered to the top so it looked like Santa Claus was riding the shuttle. He'd turn off the air pump while he was at work, though, so the Santa would slump forward, deflated, and lie there with his face smooshed into the roof and his arms dangling over the sides. Some guys from school saw it and thought it looked like Santa hugging a giant dick. They kept asking if it turned me on. I didn't answer, so one of them stabbed me in the arm with a mechanical pencil and got detention.

My dad and his friends always talk about wanting to have sex in space. Not with each other, of course, but with some hypothetical woman. Preferably one half their age, with H-cup breasts and a rail-thin waist, who can somehow still walk. Their voices get all warm and round and throaty when they talk about it. My dad hasn't had a girlfriend since the second divorce, but he is on a few dating apps. He likes to scroll through them and try to figure out whether the women whose profiles he sees have all their teeth. I don't know what he thinks he's going to do with those teeth, but it's very important to him. Recently he's also started talking about wanting to skip the dating apps and have Matrix sex with VR catgirls, though I'm not positive he knows what a catgirl is. He always makes sure I and Tony are within earshot when he does this, like he's trying to prove something or maybe trying to set an example. One time, he said he had a better chance of fucking Aubrey in space than I did. I wasn't sure how I was supposed to react, so I kicked him in the balls and got swatted with a belt and grounded for a month. It was worth it.

A couple years ago there was a billionaire who died in space because his kid hacked their smart home system and transmitted

MY DAD BOUGHT A SPACE SHUTTLE

the airlock open code from the surface. Unfortunately he wasn't one of the Lex Luthors, but probably one of their friends. My dad spent a day yelling at customer support on the phone to help him unpair his shuttle from his smart home system. I'm not that good with computers, but he figures, better safe than sorry. He likes to complain about not being able to start the dishwasher from space. He says it makes him look bad.

My dad wants to be like the Lex Luthors, in the sense that he wants enough money to do whatever he desires, and he wants a million strangers to jump to his defense whenever someone criticizes him online. What I don't think he realizes is that he's already like them, just in a different sense. They might be rich enough that they're above the law and no one alive can hold them back, but they still get old and they still die. They might have legions of people who worship them, but it doesn't change who they are. All they do is run. First to the penthouse, then the dozen mansions, then the superyacht, then space, then an entire virtual world just for them, if they can manage it. It's like they're convinced that if they hoard enough, and spend enough, and run far enough, then eventually they'll be able to look in the mirror and see someone who isn't them; someone who's above not just the law, but life and death and humanity itself. My dad does the same thing, just on a smaller scale. Nothing he buys is gonna fix who he is. It's just gonna keep making him more and more isolated and resentful while he keeps having to find room in the house for all the crap he buys to fill the void. But God damn it, he's gonna keep trying.

I'm like the Lex Luthors myself, in another sense. I hate what I see when I look in the mirror too. I see a girl, dressed as a boy, surrounded by people who hate her just for existing. The difference is that I'm not running away from it. I'm trying to fix it. I might take years. It *will* take a lot of sacrifice. But every so often, during those 5 days a year when I sit in the neglected ruins of my dad's man cave and try to work up to being who I am without pretense,

M.SHAW

I can see a glimmer on the horizon. Every so often I look in the mirror before I have to wipe everything off and I see something that makes me think, "Okay. Maybe. Just maybe." Maybe I can see a future where both of us get what we want: he'll be himself, miserable in space, and I'll be myself, content on Earth. If I can just have that, then whatever time I've got here, in whatever ways the world goes to Hell while I live it, maybe that could be enough. Until then, I count the days and watch the shuttles launch, and think about how they look so small from down here.

THE CURE FOR LONELINESS

I'M PRETTY SURE I'm photosynthesizing. That's what I mean when I say this year made me a *real* plant lady. I promise this isn't another weird quarantine derangement thing, like losing track of time or holding conversations with taxidermy. I still need to eat, but not much. I rarely get hungry unless I stay indoors too long, and if that happens I can just munch down a raw potato and I'm fine again. It doesn't have to be a potato; it can be just about anything, but potatoes are cheap and they stay good for a long time. I'm saving a ton on groceries, so that's a plus.

I wish I could point to some spectacular origin story that set this in motion. A sudden total eclipse of the sun, bite from a radioactive aphid, a fairy who sprinkled magic dust on me and my houseplants, anything. Flashy problems must have flashy causes, right? But all I've got is that I took a cutting from a philodendron and stuck it in a jar of pickle juice instead of water. I knew this made no sense and would probably kill it, but what can I say? I did it anyway. Happy Plague Year.

In my defense, I was freshly out of a three-year relationship with a guy who refused to let it go, and I was figuring out telecommuting at a company that was visibly teetering on the brink of bankruptcy. My rent was about to go up, and I had debt collectors blowing up my phone, mostly over the loans I'd taken out to get the degree that got me the job that was about to vanish, and there was an election or something, and, and, and. The hierarchy of needs had been replaced with a hierarchy of worries, with *immediately life-threatening* at the base, *potentially life-threatening* above that, and everything else somewhere above those. I never figured out what the other tiers should be. I couldn't devote much thought to such paltry, non-life-threatening concerns.

"Does your plant have a hangover?" you asked me when you saw it in the background of our office's twice-weekly Zoom call. The cutting sat on the windowsill with two others from the same plant. Three jars with a few spade-shaped leaves poking out the top, two full of water, one with pale green brine.

"It's a philodendron," I said.

"Those forever vines?" you said. "The ones that keep growing and are impossible to kill?"

"Oh, you can kill them, believe me," I said. "I'm just fucking around with some cuttings. Just to see what happens." Not strictly true, but it was a more pleasant explanation than *my mind is mush and I barely have any idea what I'm doing at any given moment.*

"Science!" you said. Not to blame you for anything, but hearing this made it a lot easier to believe, in the ensuing months, that I was conducting a cute little experiment and not ceding the entire ecosystem of my life to something I still barely understand.

I left the cutting there for a couple months, soaking up the sunlight and, presumably, the salty dill swill. I'd like to say I noticed when, against all odds and biology, it started putting out roots. I didn't notice, though, because my cat died.

Henry was thirteen. Not *old* old for a cat, but oldish. No health problems, no accidents, he just dropped in the middle of the floor one day and that was that. I called the vet, who said it sounded like heart failure, and that, unfortunately, I would probably never know exactly why it happened. And so, on top of everything else, I now had a dead cat in a plastic bag in my freezer with the city in lockdown.

I would not have known how to handle this even before the pandemic. When I was a kid, we had outdoor cats; they didn't exactly die on us, just went out the door one night and didn't come back. Henry was my first house cat. I lived on the 3rd floor and lacked anywhere handy to bury him. There wasn't anyone nearby who could cremate pets, and I wasn't willing to entertain the idea of throwing him in the Dumpster. He was my cat, not a lidless Tupperware container.

In the end, I basically *had to* take him to my friend the taxidermist, because it was either that or hold a Viking funeral in the courtyard, and I wasn't looking to lose my deposit.

THE CURE FOR LONELINESS

I dropped Henry off at Cate's in a Styrofoam cooler full of ice packs. For some godforsaken reason, I texted my ex, Graeme, about it on the walk home. Not a long message, just a simple *Henry died*, no elaboration, no fishing for sympathy. Over the next forty-five minutes, he sent eight responses, which I resolved not to look at until I was good and high. The preview in my notifications said *I wish you'd* . . . That was enough to tell me this was going to be another saga. A *Graemergency*, I used to call them, back when they were merely tiresome and not borderline abusive.

The first full text was, *I wish you'd told me sooner. He was my cat too.* (false) *I know things have been rough with work, and I know we didn't exactly part on the best terms last month, but I'm a human being with needs too and I wish you'd show some consideration for that. I didn't even get to say goodbye, how do you think that feels?*

This was both the shortest and kindest of his texts, all of which I read to myself in Christian Bale Batman voice half a joint into the evening, cackling wildly in response, with some goofy action movie blaring in the background. This had become more or less the nightly ritual, usually minus the dramatic text reading. The reading made me miss a bunch of scenes, so I ended up watching the movie twice, like a completely normal person.

That first text was also the only one that had anything to do with Henry. The rest were his usual one-two punches of anger and self-pity, which was good because it gave me full license to delete them all.

He sent several more flurries over the following days. Sometimes I looked, usually, I didn't. A body can only take so much dry-heaving over memories of drunken fights about meaningless crap, can only pace the apartment in exasperation for so long before getting foot blisters. *You really aren't gonna respond?* he texted the next day. *You're just gonna drop that bomb on me and then ghost? WTF is wrong with you?* As if it were his cat that had died. As if Henry's death were something that I was doing to him.

I doubt I've ever explained this at work, but something about my dating style has me perpetually getting rescued from a broken relationship with one douchebag, by another guy who seems kind at first but eventually becomes the next douchebag I need rescuing from. Once they notice that I have my own opinions and, god forbid, my own flaws and that maybe I don't want to be rescued from those things, they always turn asshat. I guess men just like the broken version of me better, and Graeme was no exception.

Going through the end stage of that whole process was particularly rough in this case, with no opportunity to find that next knight in conditionally shining armor. I went on a minor bender until his bombardments finally scaled back to the levels I'd come to expect since the breakup. The bosses weren't too happy with my job performance, as you may have noticed, but that wasn't life-threatening, so whatever.

Two weeks later, I brought home my stuffed, dead cat and made a spot for him on a high shelf full of spider plants. He'd spent a good deal of his life trying to climb up there to eat the plants, so it seemed fitting.

"You're a jungle cat now," I told him, and then made a series of high-pitched *rawr* noises, which he appreciated stoically. "Welcome to the jungle," I sang in falsetto, "we've got spider plants." I went through the rest of the song, replacing most of the nouns in the lyrics with either *plant* or *cat*. During the bridge, I did a power-slide across the carpet, earning me a broom handle thump from my downstairs neighbor. "You know where you are? You're in the jungle, baby! You're gonna meow!"

Stuffed Henry said nothing about any of this, but I liked to think he was enjoying the foliage. I knew that anyone who saw me doing this would think I had lost my mind, which was probably true, but I was learning to live with that. Nobody was going to see it anyway, life having become the one-woman show that it was. *The Plant Lady Monologues.*

Before the pandemic, I owned a large number of plants. Quarantine had changed this, in that I now owned a *very* large number. All 428 square feet of my south-facing apartment smelled like chlorophyll. It wasn't necessarily that I thought plants were better company than people; I mean, I didn't *not* think that, but I knew they weren't some kind of cure for loneliness. They were just what I had to work with.

If the dead cat stuff and the annoying ex stuff distracted you from the fact that I'm supposed to be telling a story about a philodendron cutting that I stuck in a jar of pickle juice, that's fair. I was distracted too. I have no sense of what happened to those

THE CURE FOR LONELINESS

cuttings during the month after I stuck them in their jars. All I know is that, when I finally came back to them, the one in pickle juice had rooted and the other two were dead.

"Weird," I said, distantly, about this non-life-threatening development. While the plant I'd taken it from was a healthy, unremarkable green color, the pickle juice had turned the cutting pale, almost white with just a drop of green pigment to spice it up. The stem was covered in shiny, hexagonal plates that looked like scales.

I threw out the dead ones, then tried to pot the mutant. It seemed like it wasn't meant to exist, but what could I do about it? Call the police? Besides, it was finally taking my mind off Henry and Graeme.

The cutting didn't want to come out of the jar. A gentle tug wouldn't move it, so I gave it a more forceful yank. Still no luck. I noticed, then, that its spindly roots had stuck themselves to the sides of the jar with these suction cup tips, like octopus tentacles. "Very weird," I affirmed.

I did what any sensible person would do: put on my mask, grabbed the broom and dustpan, and went down to the street to look for the remains of broken car windows.

"It likes glass," I told Stuffed Henry, figuring I owed him an explanation for why I was sweeping shattered pieces of auto glass into a headless Garfield cookie jar that I'd decided was going to be a flower pot now. "This is not a real cat," I assured him. "You are a real cat." I booped him on his dry, dead nose. "I would never put plants in you."

I held the pickle jar over Garfield's decapitated torso and hit it with the meat tenderizer. The pickle juice spilled in, and I lowered the cutting into its new bed of glass. I couldn't push it down very deep, but thankfully the stem was rigid enough to stand up anyway. "That's what she said," I muttered, in response to no one having said anything.

Graeme started up again that night with a diatribe about how poorly I'd treated him when he passed out drunk and peed on the floor at my birthday party. I texted him back a picture of the plant. *What do you know about philodendrons?* I asked.

WTF does that have to do with anything? he responded. Then, *What's a philodendron?*

"You seeing this?" I said to Stuffed Henry. "If I didn't know any better, I'd think he doesn't actually care about what's going on in my life." *It's what you're fucking looking at bro,* I texted.

How was I supposed to know that? he responded.

Context cues, I told him.

You're being a bitch, he texted.

I didn't give him anything after that, but I got another essay the next morning. *I'm sorry I called you a bitch. I don't know what's wrong with me these days. I'm just so lonely without you here, I don't know how to cope, and I guess I'm acting out. It's really hard quarantining alone. Truce?*

"Guess you shouldn't have dumped me then," I said and tossed my phone onto the bed. "Right?" I said to Stuffed Henry. "If he didn't want to quarantine alone, he should have treated us better."

Stuffed Henry said nothing.

I couldn't possibly eat enough pickles to keep the mutant's roots brined, and it was no longer willing to drink normal water. If I didn't put any pickle juice in, then the roots seemed to start absorbing the glass itself, which made the plant turn translucent and brittle. I was worried it would shatter if I let that go on, and then where would I be? What would happen to *Science!*?

Thankfully, it wasn't long before I found a suitable substitute. Dill pickle flavored Bloody Mary mix was at least brine-adjacent and came in bottles by itself at the supermarket. The mutant proved more than willing to partake, and it wasn't long before I noticed new leaves sprouting. Pink ones that made me sneeze when I sniffed them.

"Gesundheit," I told Stuffed Henry.

It was around this time that I started to notice I was forgetting to eat. Graeme started begging me to at least let him order me some takeout and eat it with him on Facetime. I knew better than to accept, but it did occur to me when I got the text that I couldn't remember the last meal I had.

"Do you get those?" I asked you while we were waiting for everyone to join the work Zoom. "Days where you don't eat because you never realize you're hungry?"

"Eat? No," you said. "Change outfits, though? I've been taking this same shirt on and off for a week."

"Pretty much the same thing, right?" I said.

THE CURE FOR LONELINESS

"I guess." You frowned. "I mean, you don't look starved or anything, so clearly you are eating. It's just easy to lose track nowadays."

I nodded, but the truth was that I wasn't eating. Not much, anyway. Despite my non-response, Graeme had ordered me a Pad Thai, anyway. A few forkfuls of noodles and I was stuffed. Couldn't fathom trying to eat any more for the rest of the day, and it would be a couple more days before I thought about food again. But, like you said, I looked fine. Great, in fact. My reflection in the mirror was practically glowing. I looked like a shampoo ad. My lack of appetite was probably bad, but who was I to argue with my own reflection?

In the Bloody Mary mix, the mutant's scales turned a disturbingly fleshy pink. I decided to try more fluids. It was not comforting to share an apartment with something that looked like a cross between an iguana and a small intestine. I couldn't simply dispose of the plant, though. Like my skin and hair, it was thriving against all odds, and I had to assume there was some connection. Nothing else in my life was going as well as my little horticulture project. The only option was more science.

Staying on theme, I added Margarita and Piña Colada mixes to my next grocery order. Then I swung by the liquor store for some tequila, because I did want to use some of the mix to make actual Margaritas, just, you know, since I had the supplies. I might not have been eating for sustenance anymore, but booze and weed were another matter. I had to stave off existential dread somehow.

I took more cuttings from the mutant plant. When I couldn't manage to snap the leaves off by hand or with pruning shears or with the serrated kitchen shears, I went for the hacksaw and that did the trick. I took three: one for each of the new fluids and one to try in classic old water as a control. I also moved the original mutant into the closet. Looking at its intestinal pinkness made me uneasy, so I convinced myself this was another experiment. With light, you know, to see if it still needed any.

"Yeah, I dunno what's gonna happen to it in there," I told Stuffed Henry in the pseudo-baby-talk I'd used for him when he was alive. "Maybe it likes the dark. I better not see you snacking on those cuttings, though. Not for kitties, capeesh?"

Within a few days, the one in the water was clearly dying. On a whim, I filled an eight-ounce mason jar with tequila and stuck it in there. "Can't hurt at this point," I told Stuffed Henry.

The one in the marg mix turned green again and started growing like it had just hit puberty, but it was the piña colada one that got really interesting. It went completely white and became . . . *puffy* would be the word, I suppose. Like an overstuffed chair. There were gaps between the scales where it swelled, and the soft matter underneath had a shimmer to it. I started finding clear droplets on the leaves each morning, but they weren't dew. They were slick, like oil. It started to smell strongly of pineapples.

Whatever had happened to the mutant, it seemed to have developed the ability to feed on virtually anything except water and dirt. This was good for the plants because any sense of a daily or weekly routine was deeply in the toilet for me. The only thing that happened with any regularity was Graeme's griping about how lonely he was, and he didn't seem to know any particular schedule either. I'd get a text, then start thinking about something else, and the next thing I knew, two days would have passed and I'd have a stream of unread follow-up texts waiting for me.

"I think quarantine is fucking with me," I said to you. "Are you getting this? Losing track of whole days, like you're so completely on auto-pilot that you're not even conscious?" Then I realized I wasn't on Zoom, and I wasn't talking to you, I was talking to Stuffed Henry while watering the spider plants on his shelf with a jar of what smelled like pee. I threw the jar in the trash and neither I nor Stuffed Henry ever spoke of the incident again.

The cutting in the tequila started growing, of course. Within days (or what seemed like days) it had thorns, not just on the stem, but on the leaves as well. Just above the roots, it had swollen into a round bulb with little ridges running up and down its length. Like it was evolving into a cactus before my eyes. Between me and the plant, I ran out of tequila pretty quick, which didn't turn out to be a problem for the plant. Just when I was thinking of making another liquor store trip, I found that its roots now penetrated the bottom of the jar and sunk directly into the windowsill.

"Whatchoo think of that?" I said to Stuffed Henry, who said nothing. Graeme, on the other hand, texted me three times in a row. If only I could shove him in the closet and forget about him like a gross-looking houseplant.

THE CURE FOR LONELINESS

Then I remembered: the plant in the closet! I hadn't checked on it in . . . how long? I didn't even know what month it was anymore. Hell, I could barely discern meaning from the numbers on my phone screen that were supposed to indicate the time. 3:42? 3:42 what? What even was that, and how had I not noticed the vines with oblong, jet black leaves like piano keys poking out around the closet door frame?

I found myself in front of the closet, my eyes clouded with tears. But not, you know, emotional tears. My throat itched. I'd never had allergies but imagined this was what it felt like.

I opened the closet door a few inches and looked in for half a second before slamming it shut again. This was what I saw: the plant, which looked nothing like a philodendron anymore, had gone wild. Like the tequila plant, it had broken free of its pot and had roots growing into whatever was available. It had propagated itself, spawning several variants with different characteristics depending on what the roots latched onto. Most were black and shiny, or iridescent like an oil slick. They all had these growths or blooms or something all over them too, with what I could only describe as chunky petals. I wasn't sure if the blooms were flowers or some kind of fungus; either way, the air in the closet was thick with miasma that might have been pollen or spores.

I sank to my knees, overtaken by a coughing fit, as soon as I shut the door. Ran to the bathroom and buried my face in a wet washcloth. Drank water. Drank more water. Took one of every antihistamine I had. Spent the next half hour sitting in the shower, drinking Bloody Mary mix straight from the bottle like it was a cool, normal thing to do.

I took stock of what I had stored in the closet that the plant was now apparently feeding on. There was a yoga mat. A bunch of painting supplies. A box of dead electronics: spent lightbulbs, an old laptop that had murdered its hard drive, a couple phones with broken screens, dead batteries, power cables for gadgets I didn't have anymore. A few board games, mostly unplayed.

"What's it doing in there?" I asked Stuffed Henry, who said nothing.

I spent a day or two (or maybe it was just an hour or two) wondering what to do about Closet Plant. I got a text from Graeme that said *Do you even care about what's happening to me?* And responded with a photo of the tequila plant and a thirty-second recording of me laughing. *Am I supposed to know wtf that is?* He texted. *Are you gaslighting me?*

Over the next few days, the allergic reaction went away on its own. I avoided opening the closet, which was easy, given that it was full of things I didn't want to look at.

To be clear, I knew this was weird, and I knew it was a problem that I wasn't addressing in any way that didn't also exacerbate the weirdness. My thought process was—and hear me out, here—so what? Here I was, trapped in a country driven mad by pestilence, with *plenty* of other things to worry about. How to stay fed, what I was going to do if (when) I lost my job, an internet full of conspiracy theorists who thought the vaccine was going to make you autistic and/or eat babies. Which worry was I supposed to deal with first, and how was I supposed to put weird houseplants above any of them?

When the allergies quit, I noticed that whatever was going on with the philodendrons had spread to other plants as well, possibly thanks to whatever I'd released from the closet a few days earlier. Most had opalescent nodules dotting their leaves and all had picked up the eccentric feeding habits. A geranium that lived on the bookshelf by the window had reached out and grabbed *Water for Elephants*, which now had a large hole in the center of each page. The jade plant in the kitchen had dropped a leaf into an open tin of coffee, where it was growing up rapidly into something with scores of tiny pink flowers that smelled like burnt sugar.

"I gotta be honest with you," I said to Stuffed Henry. "I don't think I'm in control of the situation anymore."

Stuffed Henry made a muffled grinding sound.

"What?"

He made it again. It was so quiet, I could easily have assumed it was coming from outside the apartment, maybe someone a couple floors up flushing a toilet. But I was standing right in front of him, and I could hear that he was the source.

"One more time," I said.

Stuffed Henry indulged me and even managed to turn his head a quarter-inch to one side.

Of course, the spider plants he shared a shelf with were

THE CURE FOR LONELINESS

changing, too. Of course, they had grown roots into Henry. Of course, they had.

"Shit." I wrestled him away from the plants, snapping the roots in my hands. I knew I was only slowing them down; the pieces of root under his skin would grow new plants before long, but he was still my cat. I carried him gently into the bathroom, the only room with no plants, shut the door, turned off the light, sat on the floor, hugged my dead cat, and cried.

I couldn't do this. The books, the crap in the closet, that didn't matter, but I wasn't ready to lose Henry again. I hadn't been ready to lose him in the first place. I hadn't been ready to lose any of this: my friends, my boyfriend, my cat, my plants, all the things I had piled into my life to remedy my loneliness.

Years ago, I'd worked out a method for this. The theory was that if I just kept acquiring more and more things and people to care about me, and for me to care for in return, then it would hurt less when some inevitably abandoned me. Which they would. I'd long since accepted that reality, but as long as I stayed ahead of the curve, there was no way I could lose them all. I'd always have something left. That system had now failed. All I had were the few coworkers I saw on Zoom twice a week, and I didn't get the sense that they'd stay in my life for all that long.

Eventually, I pushed enough tears out to pull myself together. I stroked Stuffed Henry's preserved fur, uncanny in the way it was simultaneously so lifelike and so inert. In the dark, it was easy to imagine that I could feel him moving under my touch the way he used to. "I'm sorry," I said. "I'm so sorry. I didn't mean for this to happen."

I couldn't hide forever. I stood, turned the light back on, and opened the door. I didn't know what to do about the plant situation, and I sure as hell wasn't going to be getting my deposit back on the apartment, but I had to figure something out, and I wasn't going to do it in a dark bathroom.

I went to pick up Henry and stopped. His fur was gone. He barely looked any different, but now that I'd calmed down, I could see it. The fibers coating his body were the same color, but with a slight, greenish tint. Some of the color had come off under my fingernails, and there was now a bright green patch between his ears, where I'd been scratching. It was some kind of plant tissue, coated in a film of pollen or mold or something that made it look orange and white.

I held the stuffed cat before my face and looked into its glassy eyes. "You weren't just eating him," I repeated. "You were . . . moving him somehow." I remembered hearing about a fungus that would take over the bodies of insects, eating them from the inside and making them climb trees to distribute more spores. Was this something like that? "Did you think he was a live animal? Were you trying to get him to take you somewhere?"

Stuffed Henry produced the increasingly familiar muffled grinding sound.

"What the fuck," I whispered.

Suddenly, the apartment felt a lot less empty. Over the past few months, I'd grown used to the endless, multi-sensory buzz of the city fading into a kind of white noise that implied the presence of life, but never quite confirmed it. Music heard through walls, phone calls that let me know to collect my groceries from the vestibule, the endless doomscroll of social media. People were always nearby, but they were never here; at least, as long as you didn't consider plants people. I got the sense that I was about to lose that distinction.

Whatever had gotten into my apartment, whatever was making my plants change like this, it was aware of me. This was way beyond convincing myself that they'd grow better if I talked to them. These plants were acting like they could hear and see me the way people could. Not only did it seem like they were trying to communicate, but they were also trying to get ambulatory and go do who-knew-what. And what was I going to do about it?

As I contemplated the options, something made me stop and look at the big picture for a moment. Specifically at the fact that I was only a little bit freaked out by this. Granted, I had shut myself in the bathroom to cry because my dead cat's fur had turned into stamens or something, but leaving the initial shock of that aside? The whole thing only registered as maybe moderately disconcerting, at worst. Sudden plant sentience was an unexpected development, but so what? As far as I could tell, they weren't going to kill me or anyone I cared about. They weren't going to raise my rent or take away my income. They sure as hell weren't going to harass me with self-righteous text message novels at all hours. So what was there to worry about, really?

THE CURE FOR LONELINESS

I opened the bathroom door. "Okay," I addressed the plants collectively, "I would have preferred we make a deal that involved you leaving my cat alone, but since that ship has sailed we'll have to figure something else out. I'm ready to talk. Are you?"

The closet door rattled.

"I was afraid of that," I muttered. I popped a Benadryl, pulled my thickest HEPA-filtered mask over my face, and went to address Closet Plant directly.

Opening the closet made my eyes water, but otherwise, the mask seemed to be doing its work. My vision was an impressionistic blur through which I could see the multicolored mini-jungle, already much thicker and more varied than the last time I'd looked. The previous contents of the shelves had been almost completely devoured, leaving the roots to chew on the drywall itself and whatever else was behind it.

"First things first," I said, squinting through the haze. "I'd prefer to still have electricity and running water. You may not like water anymore, but I do, understand? So stay away from the pipes and wires and whatever else is back there."

I heard the creaky sound of plant stems rubbing together, which, in context, struck me as being rather petulant in tone.

"You may not like it, but it's non-negotiable if you want to live here," I said. "Unless you can come up with a way to pay the rent by yourself, and even then, you'll have to play nice until I can find another place."

That shut it up. I'd never expected to be pleased with myself for getting a houseplant to be quiet, but here I was. I could tell that it did move a bit, but my blurry vision prevented me from seeing exactly how.

"Is there anything you can do about whatever it is you're giving off?" I said. "It would be easier to communicate if I could see properly."

A leafy rustling sound. The plant moved again, and this time I was fairly sure some part of it had drawn itself up and forward, toward my face, as if presenting itself.

I started to lift my hand, then stopped. "Please don't . . . I don't know, inject me with mind-control fungus or anything, all right?" I said. Slowly, I extended two fingers and reached toward the branch in front of my face.

Something was hanging from it, about the size of a golf ball. It was mostly round, smooth on the outside, with the smallest bit of give when I squeezed it. Like the branch it was attached to, the color was a shiny black, which was why it had been so hard to distinguish by sight. I pulled it closer, leaned my face down, and sniffed. There was no mistaking it: an apple. It was on the small side, but no smaller than those I'd seen growing on trees in people's yards in the suburbs.

"How did you make this?" I was barely aware of myself saying. The plant didn't respond to this in any way I could perceive.

"You can't expect me to eat this?" Still no response, but I got the message. "Okay, you're right," I said. "If we're going to make this work, we have to trust each other. I asked for a way to see better, and you gave me this. I owe it to you not to be so suspicious."

I told myself this must be a similar deal to how, if you get seasonal allergies, you're supposed to eat honey that's made locally. The fact that it's made from the same flowers whose pollen is making you sneeze somehow inoculates you against their ill effects. Maybe eating Closet Plant's fruit would help my body learn not to respond to it this way. Like a vaccine.

I plucked it off the vine, pulled down my mask, and took a bite. Nothing unusual about the taste or texture. Just your basic apple. That one bite was enough for me to see the core had no seeds, so I popped the whole thing in my mouth.

My eyes cleared up within seconds. I took off the mask and my sinuses were fine, too. "Thanks," I said. "So, those are the preliminaries. Why don't we talk about what you want?"

I wasn't sure how we were supposed to do this. The plant didn't move or make a sound, so apparently, it didn't know either. Unless eating the apple was the beginning and end of what it wanted from me. It did occur to me that it might be trying to grow plants inside my body too, but I didn't think that made sense. It had infected (or colonized or whatever) my other plants through whatever it was putting out into the air. If it wanted to infect me and that was all it took, wouldn't I be growing shoots and leaves already?

That's what I told myself, anyway. The truth was that I simply didn't care anymore. Would turning into a plant be so bad? How was that worse than sitting alone in a one-bedroom apartment

THE CURE FOR LONELINESS

harangued by constant worry about everything and nothing? This was no kind of a life. Might as well just go with the flow and become a walking garden.

My stomach churned like I was about to vomit. My head felt lighter, too. Not light as in dizzy, more ... unencumbered. My body below the neck felt less like a part of me and more like a machine that I was operating. I'd become aware of the synapses in my brain, could look at their layout and push them like buttons on a console. It was very freeing. For the first time in my life, I felt like I had real, complete agency. I could finally decide what to do with myself instead of being swept along by the tides of banal reality, the whims of shitty bosses and boyfriends like I had been, like we'd all been.

I realized that the apple probably had psychotropic properties.

"I'm gonna ... " I said to the plant. "I just ... I need a minute." I stumbled across the room and parked my carcass on the couch. I had to figure out how to proceed with tripping on an unknown substance, and it was going to be easier if I could just put down my body and stop having to make all these tiny little decisions for it. At the very least, I could lay there and wait for the effect to wear off.

It didn't take long. The separated feeling between mind and body didn't exactly go away, but the light-headedness and nausea did wear off, and I got used to the brain controls. They're much easier to operate now; no more difficult than playing a video game, even though it is much more intricate.

When I stood up, I saw them for the first time. The ... it's hard to explain. The bright people. The ones who were cultivating my plants, I think, from the other side of whatever veil separated us before. You can see them too, very soon.

I'm walking up to your building now. I'll leave the apple in a paper bag on top of your mailbox. I wanted to give you the next one, because you've always been such a good coworker, and, with the company in the shape it's in, I imagine we're in the same boat in a lot of ways.

The second apple Closet Plant made, I ended up giving to Graeme. A couple well-placed heart and crying emojis got him to my door posthaste, and he hasn't texted me since. He's no longer lonely, or angry, or insecure. He has all the new friends and lovers he could ever want.

M.SHAW

These beings, they're all around us. Maybe they always have been, maybe they just got here, I don't know. I haven't found a way to ask, but it doesn't seem important. They're all so warm, and gentle, and full of light, it feels like being in a cozy, soft bed everywhere you go. Just being around them is nourishing. That's what made me understand why I haven't had any appetite. When you can photosynthesize, having them around keeps you going for days on its own.

Oh: and I can't get sick. My plants can feed on anything now. Viruses are just more food to them.

I know it sounds weird. But listen: it really is the cure for loneliness. Eat the apple. Shoot me a text or just let one of them know. Come over to my building and we'll lay on the rooftop patio with all our friends and soak up the sunlight and feel *awesome*.

Just, please, don't wimp out. It's scary, I understand, it was scary for me too. Life didn't prepare us for this metamorphosis, but did it prepare us for any of the things that have happened this year? The way I look at it, none of the advice we've spent our lives following has been any good. Getting good grades and going to college didn't get us stable careers or even lift us out of poverty. Eating five servings of vegetables a day and getting regular exercise didn't guard our health from this virus. All I'm asking you to do is throw all that bullshit out the window at once, instead of little by little, year by excruciating year. I promise this is so much better than a vaccine. It's better than anything, pre- or post-pandemic. The only way it could be any better is if we could share it with more people.

Come on. I'm here. I'm waiting. We all are.

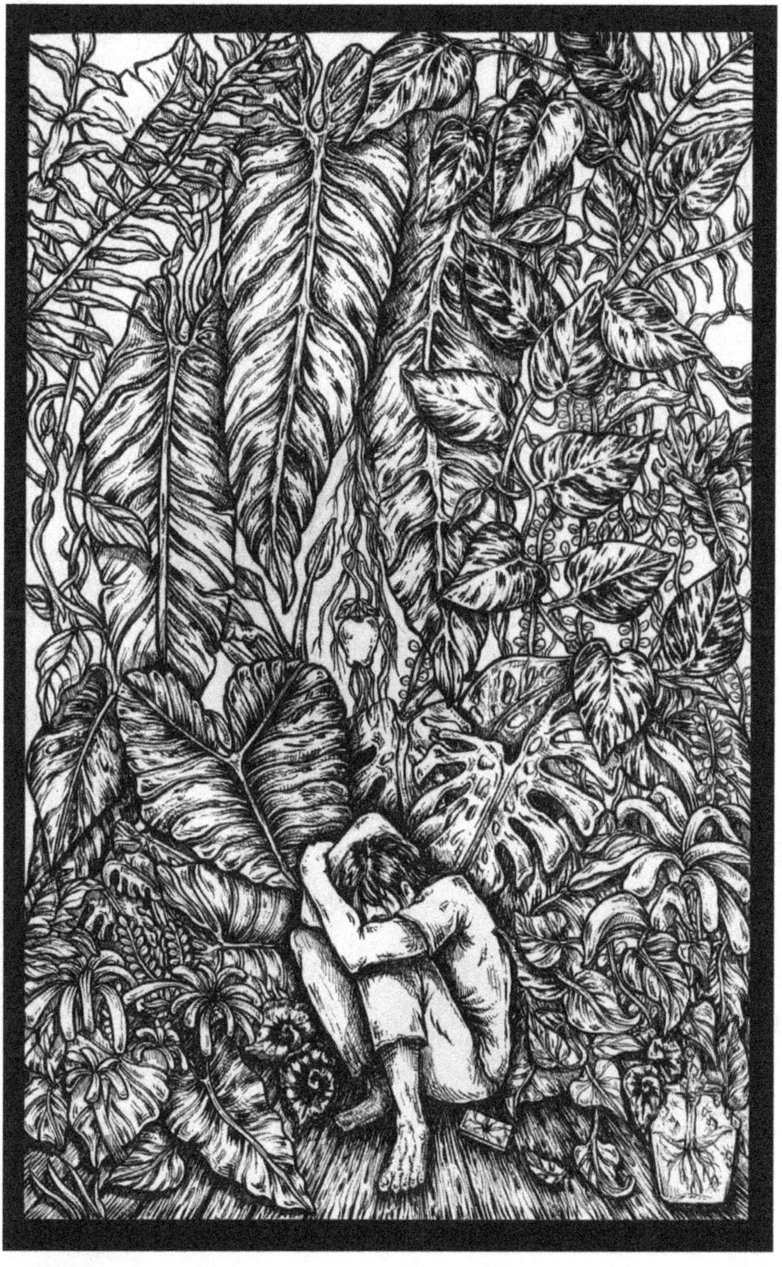

READY PLAYER (N+1)

LISTEN UP, all you sad, crusty poor people! It's me, Applequack, the trans queerdo who became a billionaire when my team won The Inside four years ago! Sit the fuck down and listen, and if you're still here when I'm done, your tab is on me! Put down whatever nasty-ass cheap shit you're currently drinking, shut up about the crummy job you're too chickenshit to quit and the relationship that you're barely pretending isn't codependent, quit looking at me like a fucking Jesus freak, and settle in! Stick a bottle of Glen-something on the bar right here, because I'm stone-cold sober and I hate it. Here it comes: the incredible, heart-wrenching, totally uncensored story of my good fortune!

Ahem. *Part! One!*

Something you need to understand about me right off the bat is that I? Am *gay*. Not the "love is love" kind or even the *Steven Universe* kind, not the kind that dresses like a normal person and just wants the bigots to leave 'em alone so they can live a normal life. I am a weird, fucked up person who likes to do weird shit and doesn't care how you're gonna explain it to your kids. First thing I bought with my prize money was a self-lubricating vagina and I'm not even a little bit sorry about it, because I like girldick but I didn't like having one, see? *That* kind of gay. Am now, was then, and long before. Don't you fucking forget it, or I swear on this little black cocktail number that my post-surgery photos will haunt your nightmares until you die.

Part two!

As you might have heard, not a lot of trans people play The Inside, because the game is super, *super* weird about gender. I used to think that was the number two reason why you can't play it at home, you have to go to one of their licensed arcades where they

READY PLAYER (N+1)

give you a full body scan with one of those airport, whoosh-whoosh thingies on the way in and make you show your birth certificate to get an account and put all these restrictions on what kind of avatar you can have based on that. Now, I'm pretty sure it's the number one reason.

I used to think the number one reason was because the profits the arcades generate go toward the jackpot. Now I think it's . . . you guessed it: number two.

Anyhoo, now that I'm done talking about pee and poop, let's get into something even more gross: how I got around the gender-weirdness and brought my gender-queeredness along in its place. See, while I may have been born cursed with a penis, I was also blessed to have, more specifically, what the politically correct among us call a micro-penis. A tiny dick, get it? It wasn't much more than baby carrot size to begin with, and when you combine that with a few years on feminizing HRT, well, there just wasn't a whole lot going on down there in general by the time I started playing. I'd already had my birth certificate updated by then too, so it was easy to slap it down on the counter, stroll right on through that body scan, and get to work. Pretty sure the employees at the arcade had their suspicions, what with me being six foot two and all, but they never said shit about it because they were a bunch of fucking cowards with even tinier dicks that they knew I'd stomp into paste beneath my size 14 stilettos if they tried anything.

In case you're wondering, these facts about my junk made it even harder to get laid than being trans does already. Gave me a lot of time to brush up on my 20th century trivia, even outside my normal area of expertise. If you don't know, I was the cartoon person in our party. Most people, I think, aren't burdened with the knowledge of how much Yogi Bear lore there is out there, or even with the simple fact that Yogi Bear lore is a thing that exists. I am. I'm the bitch who had to learn all the Yogi Bear lore. Did you know that Mister Ranger served in World War II? Explains some shit.

Where was I? Oh yeah, part one.

We could skip over the background of the game itself because everyone knows it, but we're not going to because I'm buying your fucking drinks and you're gonna listen to grandma Applequack. So back in the forties there was this billionaire who died, Garrison Deckler. Died at the tender young age of fifty-seven, despite his

M.SHAW

strict diet of pizza and Mountain Dew and all the exercise he got typing 280-character transphobic screeds with his thumbs day and night. Aside from being one of the worst people to ever exist, he was also a gamer, which is why his legacy to the world was this sort of VR video game/social media hybrid type situation called The Inside.

But wait, there's more: hidden inside of The Inside was a series of puzzles based on a bunch of 20th and 21st century bazinga-ass nerd shit that's embarrassing to think about. If your party solves the puzzles, each of you gets a billion-dollar slice of Deckler's estate. More money than you'll be able to spend in your entire life, and all you gotta do is play a little video game. What a guy, right? So generous. So altruistic. That's how you get to be a mega-billionaire, you know. Selflessness. Makes perfect sense, not suspicious at all.

Picture little baby Applequack, fresh-faced, freshly dropped outta school. She hates Garrison Deckler and the horse's ass he rode in on, probably while fucking it, and loves to post about how his grave is a gender neutral bathroom. But like most of her generation, she's also dirt fucking poor. So she scams her way into an Inside arcade and joins a party called The Midnight Orgies, which is ironic because the only orgy-ing any of us ever did at midnight was two dimensional and acquired over BitTorrent. She goes on a heartwarming journey of self-discovery with the rest of the Orgies, real *Breakfast Club* shit, but more importantly she doesn't fucking talk about herself in the third person, which is why I'm going to stop doing it now.

Part three is the one where we started doing real well on the old puzzle questline that everyone likes to pretend isn't the sole, entire reason they play The Inside, which is a terrible fucking game, by the way. Most overstimulating first-person shooter you'll ever play, which is saying something, while paradoxically requiring hundreds of hours of grinding to level up and get good equipment. And that's if you *don't* count the social media elements that make you hate your friends and family.

We started finding the hidden keys, which everybody knows by now are based on the mana colors in *Magic: the Gathering*. Picked up the red, blue, white, green, and black keys, which unlock the Fivefold Path where, if you're *very* dedicated, you can

READY PLAYER (N+1)

eventually earn the gold key, which unlocks the penultimate gate. The Inside easter egg-hunt walkthru 101.

Incidentally, getting that far is also pretty much 100% grind. You need intelligence and creativity and all that gay shit to solve the key puzzles, sure, but the world is full of intelligent, creative people and basically none of them are billionaires. Except for me. I'm the only one. Ultimately it's down to being willing to spend all your free time memorizing inane trivia, keep paying for the premium subscription so your progress doesn't get reset every month, and keep saving up retry tokens so you can guess-and-check the randomized variables in puzzle solutions. Also you have to play the game like it's a full-time job.

What am I not telling you? Man, nothing. It *is* that simple, just, most people won't ever get into it that far for long, because you fuckers have families and spouses and jobs and hobbies that you actually care about. If you want me to phrase it like some big, shadowy secret, let's just say the key is that you have to be reasonably smart and also completely dead inside. Which is also what it takes to get rich *without* beating a VR game, but I digress.

Suffice to say, it takes a certain type of person to get to that winner's circle. OuroboroSoft's whole business model is to keep as many people as possible playing the game for as long as possible, but with only a tiny fraction of them both willing and able to debase themselves into getting the prize. You gotta show you're willing to devote all of your time to a bunch of crap that objectively does not matter. Like anime. People who fit the description tend to correlate with certain other factors too: social isolation, for example. When your entire life is organized around the objectively worst form of entertainment in the history of history, people don't tend to keep inviting you to things, or caring whether you live or die. Believe me, I know what I'm talking about with that one. Or, I guess, sometimes they do stick around, but let's be real, someone who's willing to support that kind of an obsession just isn't going to make the best friend.

I'm saying that what OrouboroSoft wants isn't just for very few people to win The Inside; it's also for the ones who do win to be people who won't raise many eyebrows when they start acting in certain ways or making what would otherwise be puzzling, unexpected life decisions. But we'll talk about that later. Right now,

M. SHAW

I need you to get that there's also one critical requirement for winning that you can't select for with that same kind of addiction theory slash social engineering shit:

You can't be fucking trans. Garrison Deckler hated trans people, especially transfems. Just thinking about us made his skin crawl, which was unfortunate because he thought about us all the fucking time. He definitely didn't want us getting any of his money, even two decades after the date on his death certificate. *Especially* twenty years, et cetera.

TL;DR I wasn't supposed to get there, but I did anyway. I don't have some special X-factor or any of that shit, it's just that no security system is 100% effective. Not even an airport whoosh-whoosh box.

That's all you're gonna get from me advice-wise, by the way. I'm not gonna help you beat the game, because while I wouldn't *exactly* say that I give a shit one way or the other if you live or die, I do have enough of a conscience that I don't want it to happen on my time. Plus I signed a NDA, which I'm currently breaking the shit out of with half of what I'm telling you, but still. Beggars can't be choosers, ya dang beggars.

We solved the key puzzles, including the golden key. Yay! End of part two.

Part three!

The final dungeon. The infamous forty-three-hour play session, during which none of us logged off, convincing most people that some or all of us were on speed. One of us might have been, but mainly we were all just very sad and lonely and hungry for meaning in a world otherwise characterized by natural disasters and good, old-fashioned despair. Much like most of you little punks. Five of us in the party:

donutsthe_sexpriest, who started the party and told us he was in "sales" IRL but wouldn't get into specifics. His specialty was toys; Tamagotchis, pogs, hideous dolls, that sort of thing. In case you don't know what toys are. Don't look at me like that, I don't know what you little shits are into these days.

UbiquitousGregg, the movies guy, who was most likely to be on drugs at any given moment and claimed to be either a banker from Boston or a carpenter from Ohio depending on when you asked. Fairly sure this was an *Oregon Trail* joke, but I wasn't the

READY PLAYER (N+1)

games person so, in the immortal words of Levar Burton, there would be no *Star Trek* without transporter malfunctions.
    But don't take my word for it.
    Then there was Th3G1rl, who I'm guessing expected to be the only girl in whatever party she joined. She was the games person. Wouldn't tell us shit about her meatspace life. If any of us had something to prove, it was her. And what she specifically had to prove was that her balls were the biggest, which I was fine with because mine were already gone by then. She was always keeping track of who'd solved how many challenges or whatever and we'd just be like, "okay, The Girl." Seriously though, she was nice. She and I always used to fight over who knew more about *Sonic the Hedgehog*, a franchise that we both hated.
    Sonic is still the weirdest shit to me. I like to think weird thoughts all the time, but never would it have occurred to me that there should be this thing about fighting a bunch of evil robots, only instead of Mega Man it's Mickey Mouse, and you've got just these armies of freaky metal demon creatures being massacred by this weirdly smooth-looking rodent with an annoying voice and threateningly large shoes.
    Who else was in the party? It's like the seven dwarfs, I'll never remember all the . . . kylezDAD! He was originally the book guy until we realized that Garrison Deckler was never known to have read any books other than *Harry Potter, The DaVinci Code, The Secret, Atlas Shrugged,* and allegedly *The Art of War*. You'll note that list doesn't include much dystopian science fiction. Or books that are any good. So kylezDAD, or "Kyle," as we paradoxically called him, had to shift gears and become the comics guy, which he insisted weren't real books because Kyle was a stuck up piece of shit with far more daddy issues than his name implied. I'd prefer to think about him in particular as little as possible.
    And me. Yours truly. Applequack. Like I said, cartoons. I also shared the responsibility for TV knowledge with UbiquitousGregg, because Garrison Deckler was a weeb and most of the TV he watched was cartoons anyway.
    You got that? Okay, part three.
    Major sweaty palms, all of us. Joysticks wetter than me on molly. It's the first part of the questline where we have no clue what to expect. All of us believe at least half the rumors: that our IRL

houses are being infiltrated by the CIA as we play, that OuroboroSoft will hire hitmen to kill us if we fail at this point, that we'll be inducted into the Illuminati if we win, that Garrison Deckler had his consciousness uploaded to The Inside before he died and we're going to meet his cyber-ghost, that we're about to experience whatever the fuck the end of *2001: a Space Odyssey* was, that we're fighting for seats on a ship to colonize Mars. Look, you've gotta be a certain amount of credulous to try to beat The Inside in the first place, you've gotta be *really* credulous to keep sinking enough time—not to mention money—into the game to actually do it.

To be fair, though, most of those rumors are at least partially true.

Donuts has got the gold key in his hand, because he's basically the leader and also has the second best screenname. He's like, "If any of those rumors that Applequack was talking about in a dive bar in the future just now are true, then it was nice knowing y'all." Then he just hovers the key over the keyhole and stares at it until I'm like, "You want me to get some lube?" and then he shoves it in there like he's never heard of lube and doesn't care. He was a shy fella but you could usually spur him on by belittling his masculinity in morally uncomplicated ways.

What we get for the trouble is the UI being replaced with an old TV test pattern, the one that looks like a fucked up Pride flag with a sound that makes you want to lay on the floor with your fingers in your ears. We all sit there, staring into our visors, waiting for something to happen, until Gregg is like, "Holy shit, it's not 2D. It's a perspective thing. Walk forward." And I'll be a monkey's auntie but gotdamn, I take a few steps and smack right into the green stripe, which turns out to be this, like, pole standing in the foreground, so I step around it.

Now the green stripe's gone, the teal and pink stripes are wider than the others and they connect in the middle of the screen. I tilt my head up and down, side to side, but the game won't let me turn and I can't look anywhere but straight ahead. So I keep walking forward. Turns out, those teal and pink stripes are farther away than they look. Takes a couple minutes to get there, then we all have to strafe left or right to get around them.

Basically, the puzzle we're faced with is something akin to

READY PLAYER (N+1)

stumbling around in a darkened room, trying to feel around for the door. Only, instead of darkness, we've got bright colors and a constantly-blaring noise that sounds exactly like tinnitus. Oh, and the noise gets louder the farther we go. It's like if panic attacks were a place. Eventually we're all just staring at a solid black wall, groping around and getting screamed at. I'm like, "Some puzzle," and Donuts is like, "What?!" Which, I could barely even hear myself talking, so that was fair. I tried typing my message in the party chat instead of saying it out loud. If anyone could see it, they didn't respond.

Now, my personal interpretation of this is that there was something else underneath the endless, high-pitched squeal that we were prevented from actively hearing, but that was making its way into our brains through our eardrums, nonetheless. Like subliminal messaging, but probably more complex. Maybe something to do with the wave nature of matter, using vibrations to get into the old cranium and rearrange a few things. I know it sounds dumb, but again, I'm the cartoon person. Theoretical physics ain't my thing.

Yeah, see, this is news to all y'all. Isn't it weird how there's been a total of thirty-four winners in the history of The Inside and not a single detail of the final dungeon has ever leaked? True, we're all under a NDA and the penalty for breaking it is having to pay back your winnings, including the millions that you've already spent, but seriously, nothing? At all? Nobody's gotten drunk and let something slip, nobody's had a falling out with OuroboroSoft and spilled the beans in a vengeful storm of passion? Twenty-eight years the servers have been running. Even the McDonald's Monopoly game got destroyed by leaks after fourteen years. Food for thought.

Eventually someone finds the exit and we all get sucked into this dimly-lit restaurant lobby type situation. Kyle pulls a Leroy Jenkins and immediately gets annihilated by a gorilla that falls from the ceiling, and we all have to use a retry token.

Donuts is like, "Okay, so, no running that way."

The Girl is like, "Can somebody please put a leash on Kyle," and Kyle is like, "My name's not Kyle," and she knees him in the balls, probably hoping they'll shrink.

He's like, "Excuse me for assuming I could handle one single gorilla! Last boss we beat was what, again?" Nobody answers, but in all fairness it *was* Dracula, and he *did* punch all of us at the same time using a giant fist made out of bats, and the only way to block the attack was to take out every single individual bat, and new bats spawned at an insane rate, which was admittedly more over-the-top than a gorilla.

I'll save you the explanation of what it was like for us to bumble around in the lobby, bumping into shit and looking for secret buttons and hidden clues and shit. It was dumb. Stupid and dumb. I'll just tell you that eventually I figured out where we were: Casa Bonita. Casa, Fucking, Bonita. That's what the building where they have the *South Park* Museum used to be called, in Denver. Most people see the place and assume they built it for the museum, and modeled it after a fictional restaurant in this one episode of the show. But it was totally a real restaurant, and it really was like a shitty amusement park for shitty food that white people thought was Mexican. The *South Park* guys even owned the restaurant for a bit. Only converted it to a museum when it sunk so deep in the red that their shitty restaurant empire threatened the health of their shitty comedy empire.

I was the one who brought this to everyone's attention because, being the loyal cartoon bitch that I was, I had actually been to the *South Park* museum as part of my research. Like all self-congratulating cock cannibals, Garrison Deckler fucking loved *South Park*, so, yeah. And I recognized the restaurant version from photos I'd seen in there. I'd seen them near the entrance when I came in, and then went back to see them again after subjecting myself to the Hall of Dead Kennies, feeling the need to look at something normal like a restaurant to wash the visions of stop-motion paper craft Hell from my brain.

So I explain this to everyone and then I'm like, "I think we're supposed to go that way, with the roped off line, queue, cattle drive type aisles. That's where you'd go when you came in, you'd go through the line and order your food before they'd let you sit down, I think because the food was horrible and they didn't want people coming in just to watch the cliff divers and not spend any money."

And Gregg is like, "Cool, thanks for the history lesson. No gorillas in the bad food line?"

And I'm like, "Nah, the gorillas were part of the live

READY PLAYER (N+1)

entertainment. You had to get in the dining room before you'd see a gorilla." What we had actually seen, and were about to see a lot more of, was a human dude guy in a gorilla costume, but none of these dweebs had ever seen a real gorilla on account of they've been extinct for like thirty years and they wouldn't know the difference and I didn't feel like explaining any more than I absolutely had to, because I'm—hey! You! Yeah, you, the motherfucker with the patchy beard. Fucking listen to me when I'm talking to you, you stuck up piece of shit. I see you on your phone. I see you texting. You bitch. Now, where was I? Oh yeah. Didn't feel like explaining more than I had to, because I'm an introvert, get it? Respect your elders.

So there's an NPC at the cash register at the front of the line, waiting to take our order. The cashier has pointy ears like an elf or a Vulcan, for some reason that I never figured out. And Donuts is like, "Okay, so, what do we order?"

And I'm like, "Hold up. Have y'all seen any *South Park* memorabilia around anywhere?" And we all compare notes, and nobody has. No plaque, no printed out screenshots or animation cells hung on the wall, not so much as the words "south" or "park" in any kind of configuration.

Gregg is like, "Yeah, because we're in the restaurant version, not the museum version, right? So there wouldn't be."

And I'm like, "But the Casa Bonita episode of *South Park* aired in 2003, at the height of the show's popularity. Which, come to think of it, is probably why the episode was so famous despite the fact that it's really just a pretty standard twenty minutes of Cartman being a dick to people. But anyway, Deckler never set foot outside Canada until he got accepted to Stanford, in 2005."

The Girl picks up the torch and she's like, "So he could only have visited the restaurant after the episode aired, at which point they would have had some kind of *as seen on South Park* shit among the décor, right?" Which like, yeah, I assume, but I didn't actually know for sure. Decided not to mention that part.

Kyle's like, "So what? What does this have to do with anything?"

And I'm like, "It means we're not in the Casa Bonita that he visited. We're in the Casa Bonita that appeared on *South Park*, before the show itself made the restaurant an international attraction." Kyle's still grumbling about how this had better be going somewhere, unlike his dumb ass when he got killed by a gorilla a few minutes earlier, so I keep going. "Look, what are we trying to do here? What's our goal?"

Donuts is like, "To get Deckler's money."

So I'm like, "Exactly. In a sense, to become Deckler. To follow in his footsteps."

The Girl is like, "So in order to figuratively follow in his footsteps . . ." And Donuts is like, " . . . we have to literally follow in his footsteps." And I'm like, "Specifically, the way he experienced Casa Bonita before actually visiting it, through the *South Park* episode."

Gregg is like, "Okay, so, back to the original question. What do we order?"

And I'm like, "Nothing. Nobody orders any food in the *South Park* episode. It's all about Cartman trying to scam his way into Casa Bonita for Kyle's birthday party, which he can only do if Butters can't go. So he convinces Butters that an asteroid is about to hit Earth and tricks him into hiding in a fallout shelter, and there's this big week-long search for the missing kid, who finally gets found by someone else right as they're about to go into the restaurant. Cartman knows the jig is up, so he flips out and charges in, going through all his favorite attractions while getting chased by the cops."

Kyle is like, "I charged in earlier and it didn't work out so well."

I'm like, "Yeah, because you hadn't demonstrated that you had the slightest fucking clue what you're doing. We need to go through the cashier specifically without ordering, to show that we know the correct sequence."

So we all walk by the cashier without saying anything. We get rewarded with a bell chiming and a text UI overlay that says *Time limit extended*. And we're all like, fuck, time limit? And I'm immediately kicking my brain into overdrive, trying to remember the exact order that the little cartoon bastard goes through the attractions.

I'm like, "Shit, okay, we need to steal some sopaipillas off a table and eat them." Gregg's like, "What's a sopaipilla?" and The Girl is like, "They're kinda like a beignet, except . . ." and she thinks for a second and then she's like, "Actually, they're exactly like a

READY PLAYER (N+1)

beignet." And Gregg's like, "Okay, what the fuck is a beignet?" and Donuts is like, "It's a square donut with no hole, now shut up and start looking."

Long story short, we do it. Steal some sopaipillas, dance in front of the mariachis, watch a guy jump off a waterfall, get old west jail photos taken, look at the puppet show, go through Black Bart's cave. Each one comes with the same time limit message we got going by the cashier, and each time it makes us a little more desperate, a little more jumpy, a little more single-minded. Probably because at no point is a little clock or something displayed, so we never know how much time we theoretically have left.

After we complete the sequence, then the gorillas start showing up. At least a dozen of them at a time, falling from the ceiling, appearing from around blind corners, crawling up out of the pool's weird, blue water. They attack, we shoot. I saved the day, such as it was, again by working out a route where we could cluster together and make a steady retreat backward down one passage or another, bottlenecking the gorillas so we could mow them down with a steady directional barrage while giving enough ground to keep them from overwhelming us. We kept this up for probably a good half hour or more, never ran out of room to fall back, and never got flanked by more than one or two stray gorillas. The AI on the enemies was not exactly impressive, but then, quantity over quality.

The whole time we're doing this, I'm splitting my attention between the gorillas and wondering what the point of all this could possibly be. Because, like, as final dungeons go, this wasn't all that difficult. The gorilla onslaught was challenging, sure, but we'd handled big swarms before. Nothing quite this big, but still. The most difficult thing about it was the fact that it was taking so long, and even that was only all that nerve-wracking because we still didn't know what this mythical time limit was supposed to be, or even whether it was still counting down. Thinking about this didn't do much except make me annoyed, because none of us had slept or eaten food that wasn't in bar form for almost two days, and at that point a person can get real snippy about being asked to process new information. Every additional thing that you need to think about, every new decision you need to make, feels like, I dunno, some kind of threat. Or at least an insult. But for some reason, I can't tear my mind away from this one. So I just keep on shooting and pouting and hating life until the gorillas stop coming.

None of the dead gorillas despawn. After the battle, we're wading around through these tide pools of dead gorillas, wondering what to do next. I try taking the mask off one of them, cause it's a guy in a costume if you'll recall, and there's no dead human NPC inside. The costume is hollow. But once I've pulled the mask off, *then* it despawns. So we waste probably another half hour pulling masks off gorilla costumes, looking for which one has a key or a cashier's check or something inside. This turns out to be a dead end. We've inspected every carcass, they've all despawned, but still, nothing.

So Donuts is like, "Applequack, is there anything else Cartman does before the end of the episode? Some part of the sequence we haven't done yet?" And I think about it and I'm like, "Shit. Yeah. He jumps off the waterfall."

What other options have we got? We climb up there and jump off that bitch.

As we fall, the surface of the pool starts receding. Not like the water disappears; the whole pool, water and all, plummets farther and farther down. Eventually it's like we're falling down a mine shaft. The walls around us get closer and closer, and at that point the pool itself begins to contract so that it always fits into the increasingly narrow passage. I don't know about you, but I *love* reenacting "The Enigma of Amigara Fault" in three dimensions. When we finally hit the water, we get another time limit extension message and then it all starts draining away.

Ultimately where we are is at the bottom of a dried-up well. The Girl thought this was her moment, because she'd memorized a ton of different methods for opening fictional secret entrances. "Speak friend and enter," stuff like that. She tries poking at the rocks and stones on the wall in different patterns, enunciates a bunch of passphrases. Some, she tries over and over. Like, she says, "I solemnly swear that I am up to no good." And then she yells it, punctuating every syllable. I'm guessing this was because, in addition to *South Park*, Deckler also really loved the fucking wizard lady and pretty much all of her bullshit, both literary and political.

At this point, I'm starting to get more of an inkling about what's

READY PLAYER (N+1)

really going on. Still just an inkling, though, just a vague feeling that something's off.

None of the passphrases work. None of The Girl's methods work at all. Kyle's like, "After all this, we better not lose the prize because the time limit runs out." And we have this very heartbreaking moment of silence among us. Then I'm like, "Hey look, there's a hole in the floor."

None of us saw it appear, but it definitely wasn't there when we came in. With as long as The Girl has been poking around, as long as we've all been down there, we would have found it somehow.

Donuts is like, "I'm guessing we're supposed to jump down that hole next."

The Girl is like, "That's the read I'm getting. Except . . . hmm . . ." There's a minute, here, where she just stands there and stares at the hole, frowning. "The reference here is a video game, *Silent Hill 2*." Gregg is like, "Great, so you know what to expect on the other side, right?" And she's like, "Yeah, but . . ." And she trails off again. Eventually she's like, "Whatever, I'll kick Pyramid Head's ass," and she jumps in.

I'm gonna stop the story here for minute and none of you had better leave or go to the bathroom or anything, because this part is still important even though it's not part of what happened. I've had plenty of time to read up on the franchise, and I get why The Girl was hesitating.

Silent Hill is a survival horror series, and the games tend to be pretty bleak. Not known for their happy endings. They're about this fictional, haunted town that draws people into basically their own personal Hell. In the town of Silent Hill, you get attacked by monsters that represent your sins, your fears, your regrets; it draws you in by tempting you to pursue a lost loved one or some other goal that the town makes sure is always within view, but just out of reach, so that you keep going deeper and deeper into its clutches until it finally gets what it wants from you.

Get that? Here, I'll slow it down for you: the game keeps you *pursuing a goal*. A goal that is always *just out of reach*. Keeps you pursuing until the *town* gets what the *town* wants. Even when you *win*, the *cost* of winning is so much that most people would question whether it's worth it. Even when *you* win, or even when you lose, it's really more like the *town* wins. Like the *game* wins.

I'd bet a lifetime supply of used panties that's what The Girl was thinking about at that moment. And I'm sure the reason she jumped in anyway is because a billion dollars is a billion dollars. *Or is it?*

(It's not.)

And now back to your regularly scheduled programming. She jumps down the hole and we're all like, fuck it, and follow her one by one. Partially this was sunk-cost fallacy, but I know the other three guys were all angling to be the one who gets the pretty cis girl at the end of the saga. Not me, though. I don't date cis people. They have got far too much unexamined shit to work out, much like all of you. I just wanted the money. So I guess, in a way, we were all playing for pussy.

Also, piece of advice: your saga is someone else's side quest.

In the moment, I'm thinking how the experience of falling through this particular hole feels more like the hole is falling upward through me. Normally the VR harness would simulate the feeling of falling, which is why the arcade makes you sign a release promising your family won't sue them if you die of a heart attack while playing. Nothing like that here, though, it's just like, *bloop*. The hole was below me and now it's above me.

We end up on the surface of, like, the moon or some shit. Largely featureless environment. Dirt and gravel floor stretching to the horizon against a black background, dotted with boulders and craters and such. Oh, and we get another time bonus message thing.

Donuts suggests we split up, to which Gregg is like, "Motherfucker have you seen even one single horror movie?" Donuts sticks to his guns, though. Points out the emerging pattern with this dungeon is blind leaps of faith, putting ourselves at high risk, doing shit that should be a straightforwardly bad idea.

The Girl is like, "If we're splitting up, then everyone look for a grave with your name on the headstone," which I guess is what comes next in *Silent Hill 2*.

Gregg is like, "I still hate it, but you're probably right." And we do it. We all split off in different directions. This is fine dot jay peg.

Now, I fuckin' hate admitting this, but I do actually kind of admire the narrative design at this point in the quest. Deckler

READY PLAYER (N+1)

himself didn't do all that much toward the creation of The Inside, because he had almost no real skills, but the final puzzle-dungeon had his crappy little handprints all over it, if you're asking old lady Applequack. The guy's only talent in his sad little life, besides having Tony Stark money courtesy of his defense contractor dad, was that he was an amazing confidence man. Had half the world convinced he was Jesus, and the other half convinced that while he might not exactly be Jesus *per se* and was maybe even kind of an idiot, he was at least pretty smart and had some good ideas, which we're going to agree right now is false and never up for debate under any circumstances. He could act like the biggest dipshit imaginable in public and all anyone would talk about was how he was playing 4D chess. I doubt he could even play 2D chess, but irregardless.

What I'm getting at is that at the end of the day, a con man's job is to take your shit. The trick is, they've got to take it from you without technically stealing it; they need you to hand it over willingly, under the impression that you've got some kind of arrangement you don't really have. By the time you realize your shit is now their shit, they're long gone and there's nothing you can do about it. It's like a magic trick; art of misdirection and all that. Only, instead of surprise and delight, it just makes you broke.

A really good con man can be telling you, to your face, that he's conning you, and you still won't get it. That was Deckler's entire thing. That was how he still got people investing in all his little tech dystopia ideas after his first few ventures went belly-up and screwed over his previous investors while he walked away with another couple billion in capital gains. Hell, that was how he stayed out of jail when a bunch of kids got fuckin' brain damage because his One Laptop Per Child knockoff machines somehow leeched lithium through your skin while you used them. If you've ever wondered why hospice programs these days are stuffed full of sixty-year-olds with early onset dementia, that's it.

What was I just talking about? Oh yeah, so like, we're all wandering around by our individual selves on the surface of the Moon, looking for our own graves. Same thing we do every night, Pinkie. And I can't let go of the feeling I'm getting. I get on the comm and I'm like, "Is anyone else getting a really ominous vibe?" And they're like, yeah, but I get the sense it's more in a roleplay-y sense for them. It's ominous because we're expecting some kind of final boss or boulders from the ceiling that kill everyone. So I try to clarify: "What's the theme here?" And they're like, what? And I'm like, "The other key dungeons all had some kind of theme, right? White was all about perseverance, Red was about sacrifice and full of references to *The Matrix* and Chess and *Survivor*, that shit?"

Gregg is like, "This is the final dungeon, so maybe it doesn't have a theme. It's just . . . everything."

And I'm like, "Okay, but what if it does? *South Park* and *Silent Hill*, what's the thru-line?"

Gregg is like, "That's what I'm saying. There isn't one. They couldn't be more different."

So I start talking about subtext. And these fuckin' dweebs. These dweebs don't do subtext, except for the kind that's not really subtext. They're into, like, the Allen Moore kind or the *Fight Club* kind or, duh, the *South Park* kind of subtext where first it's like, "A=B" and then later it's like "B=C" and then you get to be like, "Ah-hah! A=C! I am very smart."

Naturally I've got a bunch of people all on their high horse about, *Oh, you're just reading too much into this*, by which they mean I'm reading literally anything into it. I just can't turn it off. I'm like, "I'm telling you, you watch enough *South Park* and you see that what the show is really about is shitty white dude nihilism, and how you're a dumbass for caring about anything. Then with *Silent Hill* it goes beyond that, and the fact that you care about something is used as a lure to get you to put yourself in harm's way."

Kyle's like, "That's a big stretch, dude," and everyone else is like, shut up Kyle, but it's not because they agree with me, it's just because they all hate Kyle. And they're right to. Kyle sucked. Even stopped clocks, you know?

"Still," says Donuts, "what's the thru-line with that stuff and the big color maze, then?"

At the time, I have to be like, "Okay, you've got me there." What I know now is that being taunted from the beyond the grave by a sarcastic nihilist was only half the point of the final dungeon. The other half was that it kept us wandering around like a bunch of town NPC's for a really long time. First we're stumbling around in a hyper-saturated Lisa Frank pixel forest, then we're doing

READY PLAYER (N+1)

figure-eights in Casa Bonita, then we're wandering around this dump.

It was never about *what* we did, it was about how long it took us to do it. Video games are all basically about dopamine; the game gives you a task to complete, you do it, your brain gets hit with a little spike of Doctor Feelgood and it keeps you invested. You haven't actually accomplished anything, but you feel like you have; just like with the subtext on *South Park*, where it makes you feel smart even though you're just drawing the conclusions it's leading you to directly. Looking back, I don't think there ever was a real time limit on the Casa Bonita level; the messages were just there to govern the dopamine cycle, making us go *uh-oh* and then giving us that hit when we made it to the next milestone.

But back to the Moon. Sweet, innocent li'l Applequack is trudging across the desolate plain, still unaware that at this point, what the game is doing more than anything else is stalling. This is why, when we do find our own graves, I'm not as tripped up by the fact that all of us find them more or less simultaneously. It feels off, but I still don't know why, because I'm still trying to figure out what it all has in common with *South Park*.

We jump into the open graves and end up in a winding hallway with blank walls and very little light. After this point, we never see each other again in-game. Being in the hallway also makes our comms cut out. So, what else can I do? I follow the hallway, which takes me to another hole that I jump down, and the process repeats. Seven jumps total, counting the grave. A few logic puzzles on the way, but they're all MENSA quiz type stuff, not too much of a headache.

If you're wondering, by the way, I'm fairly sure the seven jumps were a reference to the seven seals in the book of Revelation, which I wouldn't have seen coming because Deckler was a staunch atheist, supposedly. Maybe atheism doesn't preclude a motherfucker from thinking of himself as God, like a weird kind of fucked up monotheism.

The final jump, at least for me, involves lying in a hospital bed that slowly sinks into the floor and keeps on going. The UI goes black, then does this *Tron*-looking thing with glowing red lines that draw a series of concentric boxes. The boxes pulse a few times. Then, nothing. Then, more nothing.

M.SHAW

This is when our comms start working again. The Girl comes back on like, "Holy shit, you guys seeing this?"

I'm like, "Seeing what? What is it?"

Gregg is like, "Jesus, this is worse than a hall of mirrors. Here's your theme, Applequack: lack of depth perception."

I'm like, "I'm just seeing a bunch of squares. What are you seeing?"

Donuts is like, "Wait, I think you use the colors to judge distance here, too. I'm in a building, like some kind of cathedral or mosque or something."

I get a popup message that says *Error code 28: coagula.dll refused, fatal error encountered at* some really long numer.

I'm like, "Getting an error message on my end. I think I'm frozen." Maybe they can hear me or maybe they can't, because they don't respond to anything else I say from this point on.

I hear Gregg say, "This is wild. This is like a cyberpunk DMT trip."

The Girl says, "There's no furniture. Like, yeah, I get the cathedral impression too, but there's no pews, no pulpit, nothing."

Donuts says, "Maybe the furniture hasn't been delivered yet."

The Girl says, "Yeah, maybe it hasn't been delivered yet," with a long, drippy beard of sarcasm.

Then Kyle is like, "I'm getting a pop-up," and some of the others are like, me too.

I'm like, "The coagula.dll one?" And of course nobody responds, but saying it out loud gives me the biggest case of the oh-shits since that I've had since someone pointed out there might be a reason why *you would make a good girl* was something I used to hear so often. I'm guessing I wasn't supposed to see the error message, because it tips Deckler's hand, big time. It must have been a little in-joke left behind in the code by some engineer with a sense of humor and absolutely no belief in any kind of afterlife.

The word "coagula" is from this movie *Get Out*, which, if you haven't seen it, then I highly recommend watching it for the first time on a tablet screen, while living in your car, which you've parked in the middle of the woods because the collections goons are trying to repo it.

Kyle's like, "What the hell does this say?"

READY PLAYER (N+1)

Donuts is like, "I just heard that jingle that plays at the beginning of a Disney movie."

The Girl is like, "Where's Applequack? Sounds like we need someone with cartoon brain."

Donuts is like, "Maybe she chickened out and didn't climb into the grave."

I'm like, "I sincerely fucking wish that were the case," even though by this point it's clear they can't hear me.

Gregg is like, "This reads like some kind of EULA." That stands for "end user license agreement," which I'm explaining to you because, at a bar where they think ginger ale is Coke and Sprite mixed together, I'm not taking it for granted that you know anything.

I'm over here yelling, "Do not click agree! *Do not click agree!*" It's like I'm watching a sportsball and bitching out the TV because sports fans can't emotionally self-regulate.

But Kyle's just like, "I can't move. I don't really get what this says, but I'm clicking agree. I'm not missing out on the big prize because of some legalese bullshit."

I'm like, "There is no big prize! It's a con! You gotta get out, man, get the fuck outta here!" And to an extent, I have to admit that I'm yelling it at myself. Because it's clear to me that shit is terminally amiss here, and yet here I still am. I guess a part of me still wants to believe that there really is a pot of gold at the end of the TV test pattern.

In response I get what feels like a full minute of silence, followed by The Girl saying, "Anyone getting any clues about what we're supposed to be doing in here?"

Gregg is like, "I don't see anything like a door."

Donuts starts talking about how the whole structure is shaped like a big X, which, as you may remember from kindergarten, marks the spot. But before anyone can respond, the entire UI glitches out and changes to a black screen with the words *Congratulations! The End* in 8-bit block text. Then I get booted off the server.

That's the end of part two. Some of you look like you've got owls in your bowels so I'm gonna give you a chance to go to the bathroom if you gotta. If you go out the window in there, I swear to God that I will find you and I will kill you. With a knife.

While those three are getting their shits shat, let me explain

M.SHAW

something to the rest of you, who I assume are all schoolteachers with bladders of steel, not to mention a job that's considerably harder than listening to yours truly.

Somewheres around a hundred years ago, this book came out called *The Stepford Wives*. Or maybe the movie came out first and then the book, I forget. It's about a family that moves into this town where all the women are these perfectly docile, mostly silent housewives who totally aren't slaves. And the wife of the new family is like, what the fuck. But no one else thinks there's anything wrong, so she tries to play nice for a while. But then it turns out the women are all robots. Not only that, but the robots are . . .

Oh for fuck's sake, it came out in the 1970's, don't fucking yell at me about spoilers. Am I spoiling the precious little mystique if I reveal to you that Donkey Kong isn't actually a donkey, he's a gorilla? Yeah, that's my point, of course I can't spoil Donkey Kong. Anyone who doesn't know, at this point, I have to presume, doesn't care. You had your whole, what, twelve years of life so far to read *The Stepford Wives*, that's plenty of time. So make like a tree and shut up.

The robots, like I was saying, aren't just robots; they're robotic replacements for the men's original, flesh and blood wives, who are presumably now dead. I'm pretty sure this was a metaphor for Valium, but, like all rich people, stuff like that went right over Garrison Deckler's head, so he only saw it as a blueprint for creating the Torment Matrix.

Now, the way they explained how these doughy suburbanites were able to create such convincing simulacra was that one of them worked for Disney. Back then, amusement parks were a really big deal, just like NASA, or quaaludes. The idea was that he was involved with the Disney amusement parks and the robots they had, which were considered extremely advanced at the time because most people had never seen a robot up close and would never see another one. As you may recall . . .

Oh good, everyone's back. Damn, kids, that was quick. You must have shot the poops right outta there, like *pchoo, pchoo*. I'm not repeating any of what I just said, though. You piss, you miss.

On to part four.

From this point on, most of it happened pretty publicly. In the immediate sense, the arcade where I had been jacked in went nuts. Meaning, a lot more noise and a lot more people touching me and

READY PLAYER (N+1)

wanting hugs and handshakes and shit than I cared for. There were actual balloons from the ceiling, and I was like, how long have those been there? Do the employees have to go up in the crawlspace periodically and replace the balloons with fresh ones, just in case somebody wins? Is there a guy whose whole job is to sit up there with a tank of compressed air, reading a book and waiting for a little alarm to go off? Will there be a clown as well? Is *he* a clown? *Is there a clown up in the crawlspace?!*

Dear listeners, there was a clown. It was me. I was the clown. I just didn't have the makeup on yet.

Meanwhile, everyone with an Inside account was getting a ton of annoying notifications. There was a big ceremony in-game, which I didn't attend, where they ritually reset the questline. The Midnight Orgies, all of us, got flown out to do a bunch of TV appearances and podcasts and such. Mind you, this was the first time any of us had met in person. I don't think we'd even seen photos of each other before that. I know I hadn't, and as far as I'm concerned that's still the case.

See, the people I met in LA, when OuroboroSoft threw us a big, stupid reception and trotted us around to interviews and whatnot? They weren't the people I did the questline with.

I feel like I remember mentioning *Get Out* a while back, that one little Easter egg that I wasn't supposed to see. There's a scene in the movie—which, by the way, is basically about white America's refusal to let go of the institution of slavery in all but name—there's a scene where the main character is at a garden party with a bunch of his girlfriend's rich parents' friends, who are all being super awkward about the fact that he's a black guy. Or, that's what it looks like. Later it turns out that there's something much more insidious going on, and you look back on all those interactions from the party and you're like, oh shit, they weren't just being awkward; they were assessing the fucking *merchandise*.

What was going on at that reception, likewise, was exactly what it looked like, but also not. Mostly the attendees were all the previous winners of The Inside, plus a gaggle of OuroboroSoft execs. A few celebrities. There was this really old guy who claimed to be Snoop Dogg, even though I'm pretty sure he died in the fifties. We shmoozed. We boozed. We kicked off our Sunday shoozed.

At some point one of the guys from the first winning party got a mic and introduced us all formally. Called us up to the stage to be adored. Thing is, he was like, "Everybody say hello to the noobs: Byron Chung, Sean Sanford, Skye Boosinger, Wes Botham, and Clinton Herrick!" Cue waving and cheering. I never went up there, because I don't know anyone named Clinton Herrick, and it sure as hell ain't my name. I don't know whose dick they had to suck at the Franklin County courthouse to get those records, but it seems like a long way to go just to slap me in the face.

Byron—Donuts—put his arms up and did this spinny thing, like he was showing off a new suit. Guy with the mic was like "Welcome to the family, brothers. And sister." The way he said "sister" was exactly like a twelve-year-old boy saying "panties." Like, not only was the whole concept of sisters thrilling to him, but he was still getting used to the way the word felt in his mouth. May have been the single creepiest thing I've ever heard.

It didn't seem to bother him that I wasn't up there, but then, he wasn't really talking to me at that point anyway. I had already been getting the sense that I'd never really met any of these people before, in-game or out.

It wasn't like I tested them or anything, like by asking a bunch of questions only they'd know the answers to. Main reason I didn't was because I was sick of trivia and never wanted to recall another factoid again. But also, it wasn't like we'd known much about each other outside of The Inside to begin with. We'd been more like coworkers than friends, aside from some occasional office party style socializing on our private chat server, in between comparing notes on puzzle quests. The differences in their behavior were subtle to me. I could tell something was different, but what really stuck out at that party wasn't them; it was me.

For one thing, every single person there was acting like they'd never met a trans woman before in their life. Any of you punks ever been to LA? Ain't exactly a Midwestern country diner. Not even all that many Mormons, compared to other parts of Cali.

The standard interaction was like, some Steve Jobs-looking dude would come up to me and pat me on the shoulder and say, "Welcome to the family, bro." And I'd be like, "Uh, thanks." They really loved deploying the f-word, everyone at that party. Not my thing. I don't even use it for blood relatives anymore, for reasons that are probably obvious. Except my Aunt Starla, she's cool.

READY PLAYER (N+1)

Mostly I reserve the word for queer family, which definitely none of these people were. What they *were* was all about dropping the Olive Garden f-bomb. When I didn't say it back, they'd get this *look*, like they'd stepped in dog poop. They'd wander away and start talking to someone else, both of them looking like they'd just been served a subpoena, sneaking glances at me every so often. If the same person spoke to me again, which they usually didn't, there wouldn't be anything like the buddy-buddy bullshit they were spouting before. Hell, they wouldn't even use complete sentences.

The rest of the Midnight Orgies, though, they were doing fine. They fit right in with these motherfuckers, which was very weird given that, for example, Sean—Kyle—was a cook at a Taco Bell in Wilkes-Barre, Pennsylvania before we beat the game. I guess a lot of poor people like to think their transformation would be just as instantaneous if they suddenly came into a fortune. Temporarily embarrassed millionaires, like Sinclair Lewis put it. Unless that was John Steinbeck, I forget. Take it from someone who knows a thing or two about transitions, though: it ain't like that. Rich people live in a reality distortion field. They barely even speak the same language we do. You don't turn into one overnight; I don't care how much money you've got.

Speaking of money, here's something else to chew on. Plenty of people smarter than me have pointed out that a billion dollars is a truly fucking absurd amount of money, more than any reasonable person could spend on themselves in a lifetime. Garrison Deckler's net worth when he died was almost in the trillions. Can you imagine? Money like that makes more of itself every year than the GDP of most countries, just by sitting around in a trust fund. If the Moon was for sale, you could buy it.

Here's the punchline, though: once you've bought the Moon, what are you gonna do with it? Having more money than God doesn't make you a god. It does make it very, very hard to avoid other rich people, though, which is how I know that every last billionaire on Earth is miserable, constantly being reminded of their own mortality by the omnipresence of all this money they'll never be able to spend before they die.

I'm not exaggerating when I say they're miserable, by the way. In fact, they genuinely think of themselves as the most oppressed, most put-upon people in history. Which is important because it means, in their mind, they're justified in doing anything it takes to "liberate" themselves and get the respect and admiration they deserve. Understand me: *Eh. Knee. Thing.*

I still got my share of the prize money, my nine zeroes. I'm still set for life. You should see my gaming rig: state of the art, custom rainbowcore paint job on everything, absolutely not connected to the internet. I'm strictly a single player gal, these days.

At some point in the first few days after we beat the game, I hopped on the private chat server and told the others all about what happened to me in the final puzzle dungeon. The chat server got taken down a few minutes later. To this day, if I call their customer service, they tell me, "We're looking into it," which is corporate-speak for "We're not looking into it."

So then, at the mixer in LA, I tried talking about it to Byron. All he said was that the same thing hadn't happened to him, and I probably shouldn't worry about it because clearly everything worked out anyway. But he said it with that same look on his face, the dog poop one. He stared at me a moment, and I stared back, and then finally he gave me a rich guy pat on the shoulder and said, "Forget it, man. We saw what we saw, we did what we did, now it's time to get on with our lives."

I was in The Midnight Orgies for two years. We weren't close, but it was plenty of time for me to drop hints and dangle questions to feel out their thoughts on the relevant moral panics. They knew I was trans, and not a single one of them ever called me *man*. They may have been a bunch of juvenile gamer dorks, but they weren't fucking psychopaths.

Know who *was* a fucking psychopath? Garrison Deckler.

Tell you what, after your hangover clears up tomorrow, get online and do some research on Deckler. It's weird how basically no one who plays The Inside ever does that. Sure, they read up on his tastes in media, which provides enough material for several very boring books, but they never read about *him*. The non-media stuff. Eugenics, for example. Rich people love eugenics, because it's one of the places they can most easily find people to tell them they deserve what they've got. You're not the bad guy, it's just that everyone else in the world is an undeserving mooch who wants to take your shit.

Or, you know, don't do that research. Just go smoke a J, play a

READY PLAYER (N+1)

heavily modded copy of Skyrim, or maybe read a nice, safe book. Like Mifune says in *Yojimbo*, a long life eating mush is best. Just try to be content with only one of them.

After the reception I caught up with Skye—The Girl—on her way back to the hotel. I thought, if anyone's gonna understand how fucking weird that all was, it's her. She agreed that it was weird, but not in a way that suggested she cared, just like, "Oh yeah, super weird." I asked if she wanted to go grab some normal person food and hash out what was up. In response, she gave me a rich guy shoulder pat. She said to me, "Forget it, man. We saw what we saw, we did what we did, now it's time to get on with our lives."

I didn't know what to say, so I said nothing. She disappeared through a hole in the smog without leaving a trace, and I wobbled back to my own hotel room. I've been wobbling ever since.

Theeee! End. I'm outta here, you've been a wonderful audience, here's my credit card, try not to spend it all in one place. Momma's calling a ride share. Remember, kids, don't smoke. Or do. I've got no skin in that game. Maybe you'll get lung cancer, but at least you won't be some rich ghost's meat suit. At least you won't be wandering around in some *Tron*-looking VR environment for the rest of eternity, probably screamingly fucking insane by now. At least you won't have to spend the rest of your . . .

Back off, I'm fine.

. . . rest of your life wondering what kind of code is still rattling around in your head, or whatever the fuck The Inside somehow loaded into your brain while you were conducting a Casa Bonita gorilla massacre. Left behind, waiting for who knows what. At least you won't be unable to get away from all the other fucking billionaires, who are all the same guy anyway.

Ride share's ten minutes away, I'm gonna finish this scotch real quick. By the way, if any of you go and play The Inside after this, it's your own damn fault. You're better off in this shithole, trust me. Stay clean, support independent artists, change your underwear everyday, and always remember that the best time to buy airline tickets is fifty-four days before your departure date. Unless it's forty-five days.

Okay, quit lookin' at me now.

Bye-eeeee.

THE APOLOGY

TODAY'S APOLOGY, we have been told, is going to be nothing short of sublime. Tear-jerker. Edge of your seat. The columnists have pulled out all the stock phrases. Feel good hit of the summer, probably. Anyway, it's going to be the best apology yet. Which is a hell of a goal to set, given the amount of competition it has, from the many, many apologies that have come before.

I and Jon talk about this during the 90-minute drive to work. It's not a fun or interesting discussion, but, after only four years of marriage, we already lack much in the way of other things to talk about. I imagine any two people in the world have a set lifetime limit of interesting conversation that is possible between them, before it all settles into repetitive small talk, retelling of the relationship's more interesting past, bickering, and silence. People tell me this is just what marriage is like: a pattern that you become stuck in, often for the rest of your life, able to identify its problems but unable to imagine any alternative. I tend to feel sorry for people who believe this, until I realize I'm one of them. And so, we ask each other what we think the apology will be like, compare notes about some of the other ones, eventually agree that we're tired of hearing about it. Our attempt to cope with the routine mediocrity of the day-to-day is, itself, a mediocre routine.

"I liked the old CEO's apologies better," Jon admits. "They were funnier. I liked how he rolled around on the floor. He actually tore his jacket all down the back one time, remember?"

"You mean Wagner?" I catch Jon's look. "Relax, the car isn't bugged. We both have great disciplinary records, we're nowhere near the company's radar for that kind of thing." This would change very quickly if any of our coworkers interested in getting snitch bonuses caught us saying the name aloud, but those people aren't here.

THE APOLOGY

"If I were comfortable with it being said, I would have said it first," says Jon.

Names of disgraced executives are something you're supposed to keep to yourself. Which isn't entirely unhealthy. Everyone needs to have things that they keep to themselves, so that the novelty doesn't wear out the way it does with everything we do talk about. I, for example, often daydream about doing horrifying violence to many of the people I know. I can't help doing it, but it's fine. It's not like I would ever really do any of it. I've never told anyone this, even Jon; it's a little something, just for me.

I try to return the conversation to its former track. "I do remember when he tore his jacket, though. *Fat guuuuy in a liiiiittle coat!*" I say, mimicking two weeks' worth of memes from four years ago. It gets a chuckle out of Jon. Of course, the real joke here is that the idea of a person being fat is not funny, and the idea of a person wearing clothes the wrong size is, at best, slightly funny, and yet this phrase, repeated so endlessly in office break rooms that it still echoes in our car now, is known to be comedy gold. "It's true," I say. "Barnard doesn't use enough physical comedy."

"No, he just gets other people to do it for him," says Jon. "I mean, we all know that board member having a heart attack in the middle of the last one was staged, right?"

"Oh, totally. He was out of the hospital in two days. Probably playing Call of Duty the whole time."

And with that, we are absorbed in silence. The mistake I've made, here, is not disagreeing with anything. I have provided no avenues for I, or Jon, to try to prove ourselves right, thus prolonging the conversation. *Obviously* the board member was faking his heart attack. We and all of our Facebook friends have already agreed to this multiple times, right down to the Call of Duty detail, all of which is very funny, because the idea of someone being able to spend two days in the hospital to take a vacation instead of lose their job and fall deeply and irrevocably into debt is outlandish for people like us. It's as cliche as observing that the CEO's name can be rotated to *DURRnard*, if you're down for a little light ableism. I should have dissented.

"Of course, it could have been just a minor heart attack," I offer, but it's too late. I get nothing out of Jon, who stares intently out the window, as if there were anything out there besides more traffic. We haven't even hit the shantytowns yet.

I-70 lies prostrate before us, its surface mirage-like through the exhaust of a hundred thousand commuters. The company has paid to have all the highways widened at least twice, to accommodate the employees at the Aurora distribution center commuting from Limon, or Fairplay, or the Mount 402 settlements. Places where we can afford housing. It's still barely enough. Add an accident or two into the mix and we'll all be late, which is something that our pace today has me deeply nervous of. I know Jon feels it too, and that we are both conscientiously not talking about it. Too stressful. Nothing we can do.

To fill the silence, I turn on the radio. They're talking, of course, about the apology. This is supposed to be a music station, but they discuss current events on the morning show, interspersed with jokes about Chris and Hounddog's (the two male hosts) wives, punctuated by goofy sound effects.

Chris and Hounddog are some of the people I like to fantasize about hurting. I don't know what they look like, but I imagine them with short beards, bright button-ups, chubby hands. Guys who look like they used to be on children's TV shows, got fired, and never quite let go. I think of coming up behind them, while they're on the air, and choking them, wrapping a forearm around each of their throats. I imagine their limbs flailing as they struggle, unsuccessfully, to get free. They've never done anything to me, but these aren't revenge fantasies. It's unadulterated cruelty, purely for the fun of it. And anyway, it's just a daydream.

There is also a female host, Jill, but her main purpose is yelling, "It's a legitimate question!" in follow-up to the many clearly foolish and not-legitimate questions she asks, followed by the recorded sound of a parrot squawking.

"So everyone at that huge warehouse is gonna have to stop whatever they're doing, in the middle of the workday," the voice of Chris says, clownishly, "and they're all gonna look up at these huge TV screens, just like, what's he gonna [bleep] up this time?"

It's strange to think of the CEO's apology being material for a morning show that mostly focuses on dick jokes and stories of people humiliating themselves on the internet. But, this is what the apologies have become. Entertainment. Like a football game.

THE APOLOGY

They have pre-game and post-game analysis, highlight reels, 24-hour coverage. Bars advertise always having them on the TVs, whether it's Barnard or some other company's guy. That the apology doesn't fix what he's done, and the fact that he'll do it again, are both part of the charm. It's an emotional outlet for people. Not anything serious or binding.

"You used to work at that warehouse, didn't you, Chris?" Jill interjects between the men's chuckles.

"Who hasn't!" says Chris. "We've all been in one of them, that's how we all know how it goes."

"I know how it goes because I watch it on my phone in the break room here," says Hounddog.

"Yep. Me too," says Jill.

"I mean, yes, we all do that *now*," says Chris.

"Look, don't let us hold you up," says Hounddog, "we know you need to get back to your shift sticking labels on boxes."

The joke is that most people in the Denver area *have* worked at one of the big warehouses at one time or another, and that everyone, whether they work there or not, depends on them hiring people to do things like stick labels on boxes for a wage that you have to live 90 miles away to live off of. It's a very funny joke, because we're all in on it.

"Don't worry," Hounddog continues, "we won't tell *DURRnard* you were here." They play a clip of the CEO stumbling over his words during an interview in Porky Pig-like fashion, eventually settling on *We don't allow activities such as water or other materials in the workplace* as the phrasing he's looking for, which is funny because we all live 5,200 feet above sea level and are constantly dehydrated and can't have drinks while we're on the clock.

I ask Jon, "Do you even remember what this apology is for?" No response. He's biting his nails, watching traffic move ever slower. There must be an accident ahead. I try to hold out hope. Maybe, if they get it cleaned up quick, we'll only get our employee discount turned off for a week. Living off instant beans and rice won't kill us after that long.

The morning show hosts continue to speculate about the apology. How long it will be, how hard it will be for the CEO to get through it, what a release it will be for those affected.

"Wait," Jill cuts in, "are we talking about a boner now?" They allow a moment of dead air for silent disbelief. "What? It's a legitimate question!" Sound of a parrot squawking.

"Gross," I mutter.

Jon reaches across the console and punches the stereo's power button. Chris and Hounddog's laughter cuts out, mid-guffaw. "Gross?" he repeats. I keep my eyes resolutely fixed on the stagnating flow of traffic.

Even though he only said the one word, he intoned it in just the right dramatic, minor key fashion that I already know I'm in trouble. I should have seen this coming; I haven't been in trouble in a while, so we're due for one of these, and we've had them often enough that I can already tell where it's headed.

What's going on here is that he's going to play this like I meant *his* boner is gross. I'm fairly sure he doesn't actually believe that I meant this. Jon *is* hypersensitive about his penis, which he blames on an ex who shamed him about its smell, and on his parents for reasons he doesn't talk about. But this doesn't feel like that. The timing of the remark feels scripted, like a movie. Which, to an extent, it is, given how many times we've retread this same scenario at home. Like the apologies, it's a thing that repeats. We seem to settle it each time, only to have it pop up again somewhere down the road.

I steal a glance at Jon, and realize that he's doing exactly what I was doing a few minutes ago. He's trying to stimulate the conversation. It's understandable, in a way. Neither of us wants to think about being late to work, getting a tic on our disciplinary records, getting our discount cut or, worse, getting our purchase account suspended and not being able to buy anything at all for a while. This is just his idea of more pleasant thoughts.

If it matters, Jon doesn't smell great down there, and he's not exempt from the list of people I like to imagine hurting badly. Sometimes I imagine tying him to a chair and pulling on his foreskin. Not in a sexy way. Really pulling it back, over and over, like a rubber band I'm about to flick off my finger. Sometimes I imagine doing this until I pull it right off. *Fwoosh.* Like a sock. Sometimes, in my imagination, I stuff an actual sock in his mouth before doing this, and sometimes I let him scream. Not in real life, of course. I would never actually do any of this.

THE APOLOGY

I look into the distance, through the space between my hands on the steering wheel, and realize that this has become my life. This thing Jon's doing, this is far from new. The argument is just another form of entertainment. We've done it a thousand times before, and, while I've never exactly initiated it, I've always gone along with it. What's the alternative? At least we're only pretending to hate each other, instead of actually hating each other, right?

Maybe it's the atmosphere this time. The highway off-gassing around us, the car smelling from one too many drive-thru breakfast bags crumpled up and thrown in the back seat. Something makes me feel like this thing we're doing is what I really meant when I said "gross," not anything to do with the radio.

So, here is where I would normally say, "You know I didn't mean you," or something else that we would pretend, for the sake of civility, isn't so obvious. But I don't. Instead, I let one hand venture off the steering wheel and turn the radio back on. I don't look at Jon's face.

The men's laughter is just dying out, meaning that we have missed functionally nothing, besides the first part of a joke that now concludes with one of them saying, "Just the tip," twice.

"Wasn't the last apology about the exact same thing anyway?" says Hounddog.

"No, it was about money," Chris groans. They play the *ka-ching* sound of a cash register in the background. The joke here is that they're making it sound like a trifle among people who always want more, when actually Barnard's last apology was about our paychecks failing to hit our accounts for the entire month of December. It's funny because we're all employed, so what are we complaining about? We got our back pay in the middle of January and the apology came at the beginning of March (after a 3-week delay due to "scheduling conflicts"). Anyone still complaining about it by that point was dismissed as entitled, bitter, holding a grudge. The company's stock value went up afterwards. Wages didn't.

Back then, I even caught myself rolling my eyes when it came up. I had just wanted the whole matter to be over, after a month-long struggle to make ends meet, and another month-long struggle to get the electricity and internet turned back on. I knew, in the moment, that this had been the whole point: to wear us down until we just wanted to get through it. Even if there was no justice or vindication for us. Even if we knew it would happen again.

I still avoid looking at Jon, but I can feel the cold seethe radiating off him in the passenger seat. He's waiting for his moment, now, too. He'll stay quiet just long enough to make me feel like I've dodged the argument, and then he'll launch right back in.

The radio hosts are making fun of Barnard and his apologies now, but in a way where they're also making excuses for him. They talk about his youth and inexperience in the role of CEO and play sounds of babies whining (he's 48 and has held the job for 2 years), they complain about union rules and play sounds of people snoring while a boss grumbles in the background (we don't have a union), they wonder at how convoluted the law can be around these kinds of things (paying your employees isn't complicated), make fun of Barnard's hair and neckties, accompanied by slide whistle sounds, and then devolve into fart jokes.

Jon finds his moment and turns the radio back off. "No, nonono no. You cannot just drop a comment like that and try to use talk radio to dodge."

"I know you're bored, but find some other way to pass the time." I turn the radio on.

Punching the button makes me feel like my brain is shifting into a higher gear. I can't let him have this one. It's too obvious, too predictable. I can already trace the trajectory of the argument over the next few days, from my denial and the interrogation it's met with, to the resolute silence of the drive home, to the eventual weepy breakdown from Jon in which he recounts his traumas, to me begging him for forgiveness, to him begging me for forgiveness, to us both promising to do better, and then it all resets.

Only we don't do better. We'll just end up stuck in traffic again, with another fake outrage about boners. It's a conflict so outlandishly stupid that I'd feel silly even trying to describe it to anyone. It's beyond boring; it's become as unbearable as pretending to be entertained by yet another corporate apology spectacle.

Jon freezes for a moment. My gut suddenly feels like it's struggling to digest an assortment of various-sized rocks, or at least a gas station hamburger. Sweat pushes out of my pores and down

THE APOLOGY

my back. I need to hit the brakes. Admit I'm being a jerk, walk it back, swallow my pride and explain why my "gross" comment wasn't about his dick.

Except that I've seen that conversation play out before, too. I've tried these small rebellions, let myself get scared of pushing it further, and backed off, and what has it ever gotten me? More territory to backtrack over on the way to calming him down. Like the 78 miles we drive between home and work, I've got every boring, painstaking inch of it mapped out in my memory. If I stop there, I might as well have done nothing.

Incidentally, I do actually know what today's apology is about. The last time we widened I-70, the construction crews destroyed a lot of low-income housing nearby in order to do it. Sure, a sizable percentage of the people living there were technically squatting, and a lot of the buildings weren't up to code, but our construction crews didn't exactly have the proper permits for demolition, and there was no warning given, and hundreds of families are now homeless, and some were even killed during the early morning wrecking ball salvos. Handily, this was kept out of the press until after construction was completed.

And so, our CEO will apologize to the now-homeless-or-dead people this oversight affected. Well, not *to* them. Not to their faces. On TV. In a studio, in front of an audience of shareholders, who may be Concerned about the company's Arguably Irresponsible Behavior. The apology will be full of justifications. Who could have *known* there were so many people living in those crumbling old apartments, I mean, they were practically rubble already when we found them! Who could possibly have known so many *government* permits were required to do this, I mean, the government, you know, so much red tape, always with the bureaucracy, always restricting our freedom. He was just trying to do the right thing for his company, for his employees, nay for the *world*, and yet this went so horribly wrong, and he hopes he can grow into a better CEO for it.

There will be clenched fists held in the air. Slacks-wearing knees will touch carpet. There will be tears, or, at least, the miming of wiping away tears. There will be boasting, nested in the apology, about the company, how profitable it is, all the good things it's done for commerce. There will be hilarious gaffes and meme-able soundbites. Drinking games, around the occurrences of certain words, will be played. He will make himself pathetic—which is to say, he will make it about him.

The shareholders will stand and applaud. They will find it in their hearts to forgive the CEO. Warm profiles of the CEO will appear in the press, with photos of him embracing his family, proclaiming this the moment he truly became a leader. Politicians will express admiration for his humility. The President himself will talk about what a great person the CEO is. Fines, citations and lawsuits will spontaneously disappear, or quietly fail to be enforced. We will be allowed to go home 30 minutes early (without pay), urged to spend the extra time reflecting on the company's long-standing commitment to ethics and good business practices.

But not the people. Not the homeless or the dead. They will not be involved in any part of this process. We will all go through this knowing that there will be more apologies, very likely for the same scenario or something like it. We'll engage in the same old recreational cynicism, while we go on being, effectively, indentured servants of this hideous enterprise that we claim to be too smart to respect. All the relevant pull-quotes will be added to the next book of humorous apology-isms, featuring a goofy photo of the CEO's face on the cover, which will sell tens of thousands of copies through outlets that the company owns. He will look like a fool before the whole world, and nothing will change as a result.

I feel a vivid daydream coming on. It's happened before, this one. I imagine being in the room where he delivers all these apologies, rushing the stage, up between the rows of chairs, and knocking him to the ground. The pain I inflict in this one isn't as precise as the others. I'm just wailing on his prone, pillowy, business-suited form. Just kicking the shit out of him. Demanding an apology for all the things he's destroyed and stolen from my life. Screaming in his terrified face that he didn't have a permit to demolish my marriage. Not accepting whatever bullshit he stutters in response. Pounding his face until it looks like mashed potatoes. Of course, I'm not really this violent of a person. Thinking it, though, sure feels good.

Traffic is at a dead stop. I shift the car into park. Beside me, Jon's cheeks are twitching with the effort of maintaining his open-mouthed scowl. I start tabulating a mental balance sheet on how

THE APOLOGY

much I will pay for telling him it takes fewer muscles to smile; what names he will call me, how bad it will look when he recounts the story to others. Again, I head my mind off at the pass. I know he's going to call me those names anyway, and if he tells the story, he'll make me sound as bad as possible, no matter what I do now.

He opens his mouth.

"No," I say. "No thanks."

Every neuron in my body is rioting as I turn off the ignition and get out of the car, taking the keys with me. We're not even halfway to Aurora, and there's very little beyond the highway but the desolate Front Range, swathes of dry prairie and blighted wastes that were once farmland. I've heard stories about drifters living out here, but it's hard to tell how much of it is media sensationalism. I suppose I'm about to find out.

Behind me, Jon has gotten out of the car too. He's shouting. I don't respond. I just told him everything I need to. I keep my eyes on a fixed point on the horizon, as if I mean to walk right off the edge. I have no plan. Whatever I'm about to do will be orders of magnitude more difficult than the life I'm leaving. But the only security of that life lies in the relatively slow whittling away of possibilities. The promise that my dehumanization will happen gradually enough for me not to notice. But it's going to happen either way, and, that being the case, I might as well at least die looking for other possibilities.

Somewhere next to me, I hear the telltale click of a car door opening. Someone else is getting out of her vehicle and following behind me. With no more idea of where she's going than I do, I'm sure. I wonder what caused the traffic to stop. I dare to hope. I give myself a vision of hundreds of people on I-70 ahead of us, already doing exactly what I am doing. Of the sun setting on a highway turned into a giant, absurd parking lot in the middle of the desert, and this, I know, would be more brutal to the CEO than any physical violence anyone might ever do him.

Years later, I will wonder if this argument was to have been the final nail in the coffin. If Jon could throw a stink this ridiculous and get *me* to apologize to *him* over it? In that moment, he knows, if he can get me to accept treatment this egregious, I will never have the will to break out of the pattern, as long as I live. But in the end, I'll know that there would always have been another stair for

149

us to fall down. That the wake-up call is not so much about hitting rock bottom as it is about the moment you realize that there is no bottom, that what you allow will continue, and it will only ever grow bigger and hungrier, and there will always, somehow, be more of you to devour.

APARTÉMON

Q: None of the apps on my phone are working except this one. Can you help me?
A: Thank you for playing Apartémon, the number one AR (augmented reality) game for making New Friends! Best of luck starting your digital adventure, and feel free to consult our 24-hour chat line anytime you need help by tapping [Plead].

Q: Thanks, but that doesn't answer my question. I need to be able to look at texts and emails and stuff, but none of my other apps work. I don't even remember downloading this game, it just appeared this morning, what's going on?
A: As a social AR game, Apartémon is not downloaded through the app store. Another player AirDropped it to you while you were out walking your dog. Once installed, you must play the game to completion to unlock other functions.

Q: So it's, what, a virus?
A: No. It's the number one AR (augmented reality) game for making New Friends. Please try to keep up.

Q: Fine, how do I play? Is it quick?
A: No. Apartémon is played entirely inside your apartment. As you roam the three rooms in which you already spend 80% of your life, you will encounter various types of New Friends. You must capture and train your New Friends, on your way to becoming an Apartémon master.

M.SHAW

Q: What does Apartémon mean? Is it short for "Apartment Monster?"
A: No. This isn't Pokémon. It means "My Stage Whisper" in French.

Q: Seriously?
A: I am always serious.

Q: I met Prof Buckeye, the weird guy at the beginning of the game who told me basically everything you told me, and gave me my first handful of Apartéballs. He looks familiar. Have I seen him somewhere before?
A: If you had spent any time socializing at Ohio State instead of playing video games in your room, you would know that he is the university's mascot, Brutus Buckeye, only wearing a lab coat instead of a mid-century football uniform. He is not a real professor, nor any kind of scientist, but that doesn't matter to you! As of his visit, you are now an Apartémon Trainer, and you don't have time to worry about whence Prof Buckeye derives his authority. Focus instead on collecting powerful Friends to help you become an Apartémon Master!

Q: What is a buckeye, anyway?
A: It's the name of both a type of tree native to North America, and the nuts produced by that tree, of which Prof Buckeye's head is a giant one, with a face.

Q: Are they edible?
A: If you want to die, sure!

Q: How do I catch more Apartémon?
A: First of all, they're not called that. They're New Friends (Apartémon is a social game, remember). You catch them using the Apartéballs, which are actually unusually large, heavy buckeyes. Your existing Friends battle the newcomers until they are sufficiently weak. Then, you hurl an Apartéball at their head, knocking them unconscious, by tapping [Capture]. Finalize the capture by transporting them to the laundry closet and tapping [Imprison].

APARTÉMON

Q: But I don't have any Friends yet. How do I get my first one?
A: Your starter Friend is the dog you were walking when you received the game. You do not have to capture them, simply aim your phone at your dog and tap [Conscript].

Q: Can I contact the person who sent me this game?
A: I doubt it. They're not going to be leaving their apartment anytime soon either.

Q: Why did they do this? What's the point of sending me this game?
A: That's exactly what you're meant to think about. What *is* the point? The game may seem like a waste of time, but was walking your dog, or going to work, or scrolling through Facebook any more meaningful? Do these banal rituals improve you in any way? Do you *like* walking your dog, or are you just doing it because that's what you're supposed to do?

Q: The dog needed a walk.
A: You view walking your dog as important, but wouldn't anything feel equally important, as long as it involved meeting an obligation handed to you by somebody else?

Q: You're supposed to answer my questions, not ask other questions in response.
A: That's not a question.

Q: Yeah, I'm not really into this. I'm taking my phone to the Apple store to get rid of this app.
A: Take your time.

Q: Well, that was a waste of four hours. Can you please tell me how to uninstall? I really don't want to play this game.
A: You could always restore your phone to its factory settings.

Q: But I'd lose everything that's stored on it.
A: See, you get it. Might as well play the game.

M. SHAW

Q: I've been pacing my apartment, but I haven't encountered any Aparté... any New Friends. What am I doing wrong?
A: You expect your New Friends to just wander into your apartment without a little help? You have to attract them with food! Get some Apartésausages by aiming your phone at the refrigerator and tapping [Reload], then leave a plate sitting out by tapping [Lure]. When a New Friend comes to snack on them, initiate a battle by tapping [Blindside].

Q: During battle, why am I being given the option to [Eat] the Apartéball?
A: Eating any object smaller than your fist is always technically an option. It might hurt you, temporarily or permanently, but if you can fit it in your mouth, you can probably eat it. I just think this is something worth remembering, in general.

Q: So far I've caught four different cats, a Chihuahua, and a California Ground Squirrel. Are there any types of Friends besides dog-type, cat-type, and squirrel-type?
A: Those are the only three types of Friends available to an Apartémon Trainer. Dog-type is strong against squirrel-type but weak against cat-type, cat-type is strong against dog-type but weak against squirrel-type, and squirrel-type is strong against cat-type but weak against dog-type.

Q: I ran out of Apartéballs. How do I get more?
A: They're in the medicine cabinet. Hold the phone in front of your antidepressants and tap [Transmogrify].

Q: Prof Buckeye said something about an "Apartédex." What is it?
A: You can access the Apartédex using the computer in your apartment. It's a social media front-end that you use to obsessively create accounts for all the Friends you've collected and post photos of them with captions written in their voices. Just another of the many futile attempts you've made to remedy the isolation inherent in digital life.

Q: Can I get followers for my Apartédex accounts?
A: It's cute that you expect people to care about this.

APARTÉMON

Q: Can I do anything else with the computer?
A: You can respond to event invites you've gotten from people you claim to know in "real life," but please note that, no matter how you respond, you won't be able to leave the apartment to go to any of them. As if the idea of making actual friends is a fantasy that you can never act on. So, the same thing you've always used it for.

Q: I encountered a rat. Is it considered a squirrel-type Friend?
A: No, that's just a rat. You can't catch it, but you may have to fight it if it shows up to snack on the Apartésausages.

Q: Same deal with cockroaches? They're attracted by the food?
A: Correct.

Q: Come to think of it, how are all these dogs, cats, and squirrels getting into my apartment?
A: Remember when you moved in and thought, *I should have something done about the leaky windows in this place,* until you realized that would involve talking to your landlord, and you decided to play Mario Kart instead?

Q: No offense, but I really don't want to play this game. I tried restoring my phone to factory settings, but nothing happened. What am I missing?
A: You can't restore factory settings mid-game.

Q: But I can't get out of the game.
A: Just think about that stack of games sitting next to your Apartédex that you've given up on the moment you got stuck somewhere; this is an opportunity to finally see something through, for once!

Q: Can I look for New Friends outside my apartment? Walking up to the door and tapping [Escape] doesn't do anything.
A: You cannot [Escape] mid-game. Why would you want to? All your Friends are here. Of, course, I suppose you could simply walk out the door.

M.SHAW

Q: But the game doesn't give me that option.
A: The only options that are ever available to you are the ones you give yourself. If you can't leave, that's on you, not the game.

Q: I don't understand. Are you saying I control the game?
A: Yes, but in a way where the game controls you.

Q: Oh god, there's so many rats and cockroaches. My apartment is infested. What happened?
A: It's because you're always leaving food sitting out.

Q: But don't I have to leave food out to attract New Friends?
A: Look, no one said this was going to be easy. Your New Friends like food, and so do rats and roaches. They're just part of the whole Apartémon Master deal.

Q: Is there a way to get rid of the rats and roaches?
A: I suppose, if you were able to leave the apartment, you could purchase traps and poison, as well as steel wool and caulk and other supplies for pest-proofing your home, but that is not possible anymore. If you want to be rid of them, you'll have to fight every last one personally.

Q: Won't people be concerned that I serially respond Yes to their event invites, but never show up?
A: No, they'll figure you're just really flaky. They won't know the difference between you and their dozens of other friends who never honor their commitments.

Q: OK, I stopped leaving out food and fought the vermin until they all died. It took two days, but am I finally rid of them?
A: Nope! They'll be back as soon as you start leaving out food again.

Q: What if I don't start leaving out food again?
A: Then you won't be doing much, besides aimlessly pacing your apartment.

APARTÉMON

Q: Where is all this going? What is the object of the game?
A: To capture, train, and battle to become an Apartémon Master. I feel like we've been over this.

Q: But, I mean, what are the metrics attached to that? At what point do you actually *become* an Apartémon Master? Is there a final boss or something? A certain number you have to catch?
A: Don't worry about it. Focus on what you need to do now, not the distant goals of the future. True Apartémon Mastery is in your heart.

Q: So, what, I'm supposed to pace around my apartment playing this game until I die?
A: More or less. When you die, your Friends will ritualistically devour the carcass so that your spirit can finally ascend to the Golden Apartment in the Sky. After you're gone, your stronger Friends will devour the weaker ones, until there is only one left, who, if they are lucky, will succumb to their wounds before they have a chance to starve.

Q: Will my Friends also go to the Golden Apartment in the Sky when they die?
A: They don't have souls, so no.

Q: I've been playing for two weeks. This doesn't have anything to do with the game, but I'm worried about the fact that no one seems to have missed me enough to get in touch. What's going on in the outside world?
A: Ask your friends.

Q: Do I have any friends, though? I mean, *really*? People who genuinely care enough to check in and see if I'm okay when I drop off the radar without warning? Maybe I don't. Maybe my participation in society, or lack thereof, is of no real consequence to anyone. Even me.
A: Without you, the world will go on unaffected. You are not *even* a cog in the machine. You will never have a shred of meaning to anyone but yourself, and if you can't even manage that much, then what is the point of you? Society, and even the people who claim

M.SHAW

to love you, will never provide you with the meaning you seek. You have to make your own meaning.

Q: Who am I talking to right now?
A: The same person you've always been talking to. The one who answers all the questions whose answers you should already know, when you need the comfort of a voice outside yourself to validate the uncomfortable truths of your existence. A stage whisper. An echo, buoyed by the acoustics of the high-vaulted brainpan where you act out all these games to augment the bleakness of your reality.

Q: Prof Buckeye?
A: Apartéballs are in the medicine cabinet.

OBJECTS AT REST

MOM DIED IN MAY, Dad in September. By the end of the year, it was like they had never existed at all. The mourners and well-wishers had long since gone home and slowly stopped checking in. My little brother and only sibling lived three time zones away and we still rarely spoke, despite stated intentions otherwise. It wasn't his fault, I knew. Letting go had never been a problem for him, because he couldn't stop letting go. This was how he had always been: flighty, and perpetually in motion. Just shy of twenty years ago, he had been one of those kids you see on leashes, because he would fly away if Mom and Dad didn't tether him to themselves. He couldn't have really comprehended what it was like for me to live with their death. He had already let them go, and I often felt that he had let me go as well. I envied him. I wished I could let me go, too.

For my friends who had never met them, the death of my parents existed only as an idea. They knew, rationally, that it must be hard for me, but they never really saw any of it. My December 12th birthday came and went, with a subdued bar crawl during which I seemed no more sad than anyone in 2017 had every right to be. The birthday party-goers went home to join the mourners and well-wishers, and I went back to doing what any 24-year-old with a bachelor's in history does best: waiting tables.

The restaurant was a casual joint with booths and a bar and "Grille" in the name, part of a national chain. Poorly lit. Free refills. The closest we came to accommodating any dietary restrictions was the kid's menu. Not even the salads were vegetarian. My coworkers were a rotating cast of interchangeable impoverished youth, plus a few older cooks who did this as close to professionally as casual dining kitchen work gets. The manager was a tall, bald-headed white man named Chuck. Chuck was essentially a coward at heart who had acquired a cruel streak through decades of working overtime in high-stress environments. He knew this and tried to play off the cruelty by feeding us a lot of positive language and what he called "compliment sandwiches." Nobody liked him, but it was hard to exactly hate him because he was such a standard-issue restaurant manager that you almost didn't notice him. We might as well have been any other restaurant fitting this description. It was the suburbs; there were at least three more within a mile radius. We were never slow.

When I went to work the night after my birthday, I had begun to feel like my desire to let myself go was coming to fruition. Like my parents, who, at that point, might as well have been figments of my imagination, I could feel myself disappearing. Only instead of death, I was disappearing into the restaurant. Any inclination I'd had toward grad school had plummeted that year, I could feel my social life stagnating and hobbies had fallen off the radar. I wasn't dating anyone or trying to. Nobody needed me. Nobody was relying on me. Except the restaurant. Restaurant work is happy to consume as much of your life as you're willing to give it, and it wasn't like I had any other priorities. So, I worked 60-hour weeks bringing people their burgers and salads, numbly getting hit on, and washing marinara sauce out of a small collection of black aprons in my spare time. There was almost nothing left of *me* in me. Something in the back of my mind still resisted this. Mostly, I tried to quiet it by focusing even more on work. This was coping, I told myself. This was how I would cope with Mom and Dad. But there were still moments where I did not fully want to cope.

One of those moments smacked me in the face around the tail end of dinner rush, and I texted my brother in Seattle a *how's life*. Not those exact words, but not much more, and I put the phone away as quickly as possible. It was a 3-second rebellion against my impending, voluntary disappearance. This was by necessity; getting caught with my phone out would earn a chewing-out from Chuck, who was surprisingly stealthy, using our tendency not to notice his presence to his advantage.

I didn't know what I was expecting to happen, here. Texting my brother was like tweeting at a celebrity. He had dropped out of college at 20 years old and moved to Seattle for reasons unclear.

OBJECTS AT REST

As far as I knew, he wasn't doing anything much more exciting than me, work-wise. Whenever you talked to him, though, you got the sense that he was busy with some unknown, very exciting thing that you were distracting him from. It was a vibe that always made me want to oblige him and let him get back to it as quickly as possible. If he was an object perpetually in motion, then I was one at rest, always staying in the same city, holding onto what I had for dear life, no matter how little or how intolerable it became. I don't suppose I could have understood his needs any more than he was capable of understanding mine.

Before I could think about it in any real depth, I finally got the attention of Ralph, the cook who worked the grill station. "Hey, the guy at table 14 wants to know if the salmon is wild caught," I told him.

I could see Ralph's jaw clench. He was making the salmon in question for the second time, the first attempt having been sent back as overcooked. "Man, I don't know," he said. "If it was wild caught, wouldn't it say that on the menu?"

"He says he can only eat salmon that he knows is wild caught. His doctor won't let him eat farm raised. Says he's allergic."

"Allergic?" said Ralph. "Allergic to what? Farms?"

I shrugged.

"Why the fuck he order it then?" He swiped the salmon off the grill with a spatula and tossed it to the side. The slab of fish bounced off the side of the oven and into the trash. "Find out what he wants this time, I guess."

Now my own jaw clenched. I did not want to go back to the customer's table. Most nights, we had at least one *the customer*, and tonight, it was definitely this man. He had come in with four other people. Two couples, both on the younger side. Twenties-ish. Now, he sat at the table alone, his younger companions having already eaten, paid their bills, and left. I don't remember ever seeing them speak to him, or even look at him. He just trailed along behind, like a remora, his actual relationship to them unclear.

I hadn't really noticed him myself until all the food came out, and he looked at his maple-glazed chicken (this was *before* the two attempts at a salmon filet) and said, "I didn't order that."

This was when he had forced me to see him. His slack face, permanently repulsed expression, steeply sloping shoulders. His blue sweater, worn over a blue button-up and blue slacks, as if the police had casual Fridays. "I ordered the salmon," he said.

This was a lie, of course. He had changed his mind. But you couldn't just *say* that. So, the chicken had to go back. I should have been annoyed, as I was whenever we saw this behavior, but this time, a different type of anxiety took over. A feeling more like treating a fragile thing carelessly. Just looking at him made me worry about him. He seemed troubled, and weak, more than someone his age should have been. Like a sick dog, he gave me this urge to make sure he was okay, without wanting to touch him. Every time I replayed this interaction in my head, or any other one that I'd had with him, it felt like dropping a wine glass. Like rolling a heel.

Now, here we were again. Walking back toward the table produced a nails-on-a-blackboard feeling down my spine. Wasn't he starving, having waited this long without ordering what he actually wanted? Wasn't he embarrassed to be sitting there by himself, after his . . . friends? Nieces? Students? had already left?

He was looking at photos of boats on his very large phone when I came up next to him, and he hurried to cram the device back into his pants pocket. "Hey!" I said, "I'm really sorry, but we don't know for sure if the salmon is wild caught. Would you like to order something else?" I had left the menu at the table, not from any kind of premonition, but because he had seemed not to want to let go of it before.

"Oh. Uh. Come back in a minute," he said to me. "I need a minute. I just need one minute."

Without a word, I set down the fresh diet coke I had brought for him (his fourth) and left him to his business with the menu. Doing so carried the same vague discomfort as leaving a small child alone with an unlocked iPad.

I tried to think about something else. Like my own family matters, which at least offered a more comfortable, low-key sadness. But, as I kept myself busy with my other tables—families, mostly, the kind with younger children and living parents, and a group from an old folks' home who wanted to know if they could order crème brûlée to go — my mind kept itself saddled with the customer. He seemed, somehow, to be suffering. Like trying to figure out what to order brought him tangible, observable pain. His

OBJECTS AT REST

coming to the restaurant felt like a bid to infect me with this, to make me suffer. I *was* suffering, but not for reasons related to him, and he had no business barging in and trying to make my suffering about him.

Mom and Dad had left me the house, which I was now living in, because it was paid off. It did not feel good to live there, but I knew better than to turn down rent-free housing. It wasn't the house I had grown up in; they had downsized drastically when my brother moved out. The new, smaller house was sized perfectly for me to live in by myself.

I had expected this to make it easier, but now here I was living in the house of my dead parents, with no nostalgic attachment to the house itself. And it was full of their stuff. Their dead people stuff just as much at rest, without mortal purpose, as they were. Anything I could have had any real attachment to in the house was dead. I often wondered, if I died, who would live with my dead stuff? My brother? Unlikely. He wasn't even willing to be around my alive stuff, for any length of time. I wanted someone to be willing to live with my dead stuff, but how do you communicate that to a person? How do you find a person you're willing to communicate that to?

As I was bussing another table, Chuck snuck up behind me. He was terrified of ever touching anyone (he told this to all of us, on our first day) and would never even tap you on the shoulder, just walk up behind you and start talking. "We're comping that guy's meal," he whispered, with an audible tremor.

I set down my tray, proud of not having dropped it. "Okay."

"We made a mistake on his order three times. We're gonna comp him."

"Okay." I considered pointing out that we hadn't made three mistakes, or even one, but by that point in the night, I didn't feel like fighting him. My feet were in open rebellion and I wanted to go home and sleep before my double the next day. It was already less than 12 hours until I had to be back here. Not that I had anywhere else to be, of course.

I felt my phone buzz in my pocket and ignored it. This wouldn't be my brother, whose response time ranged between two days and several weeks for texts. That at least would be the time frame if he responded at all, which was a 75% chance at best. Probably yet another neglected friend inviting me to a karaoke night, forgetting how late work tended to keep me. Most of my friends were left over from college, and still doing more or less the same things for fun that we were then, which was starting to feel a little too much like running around the city in footie pajamas. How many times could we possibly sing the same ironic renditions of 90's pop songs? How many *hundreds* of times? I didn't have any friends from work, though, and had never really looked into other ways to acquire friends, so these outings were about all I could get for socializing, when I could get anything.

"I want to let you know, you're doing great," said Chuck. "It's not your fault. But we don't want to lose his business or get a bad review."

"Whose fault is it?" The words left my mouth before I knew it, flagrantly violating my brain's chain of command.

"Nobody's," he said. "Sometimes these things just happen. Don't let it get to you."

I'm trying! I thought. Really trying! There was no reason for me to care how much money the restaurant made, so why should it get to me at all? "Okay," I said again.

It was absolutely getting to me, though. I really hadn't done anything wrong, so why did I feel like this? Wondering about it only made me that much more anxious. I looked across the room at the customer, still looking at the menu, rubbing his chin. *Sometimes these things just happen*, the manager had said. What did he mean? What were the *things* that *just happened*? People not knowing what to eat? It was such a strange idea. As if the customer's indecisiveness were something that was happening *to* him, like a question on a test he didn't know the correct answer to. As if he wasn't actively refusing to make a decision.

As I was bringing the tray of dishes back to the dishwasher, one of the cooks called out to me. "Hey, come look at this." It was Vicente, the guy who worked the fryer. I turned and saw him digging something out of the pocket of his chef jacket.

"Hey, tell me something. Do you ever not know what to eat?" I caught the object he tossed me: a pear-shaped leather pouch that buttoned shut at the top. It didn't have anything in it.

"Man, I'll eat whatever. I don't give a fuck. After I work a shift here, I'd eat a fried rat on a stick. I don't care. Fuckin' bees, whatever. I'd eat a salad made out of banana peels. We don't get no breaks back here. I don't give a shit. What do you think that is?"

I turned the pouch over in my hand. "Is it a coin purse?" He didn't seem like the kind of person who would have a coin purse.

A flat, restrained grin crept across his face. "I mean, what's it made out of?"

Definitely something gross. The cooks loved to be gross. People cope how they can. Or don't, in my case. "A tongue?" I guessed.

The grin unfolded to its full wingspan. "It's made from a kangaroo scrotum."

"Ah." My eyes fixed on the coin purse, unable to look anywhere else. I did not want to look away from it, implying that I was embarrassed to be holding the cured scrotum of a dead kangaroo, and I didn't want to look at Vicente, because he was enjoying being gross, which is gross in and of itself, and I didn't want to see that. I wanted to look like I was contemplating the object in my hand with detached bemusement. I probably just looked nervous, despite my efforts. "Where did you get this?"

"You can't get them anymore," he said, answering some other question, tangential to the one I had asked. "They're illegal in Australia. That's where they come from."

The pouch smelled like regular leather, and I was not comfortable with that, because I did not want the smell of leather to remind me of this. I couldn't see anyone wanting a kangaroo scrotum coin purse, much less enough people for a country to have to make a law against them. And yet, here we were.

"It was my abuelo's. He left it to me."

I had thought, throughout previous shifts, that Vicente seemed nice. But then, so do a lot of guys, until they're dropping marsupial ball sack in your hand. "I bet he had some great stories," I managed.

Vicente shrugged. "He died when I was a baby. This thing was in a box in the attic until I turned 15."

There was a moment, here, when I was about to open my mouth to tell him that my parents had left me their house, and enough money to pay off my student loans, plus a little extra, which I guessed I was supposed to put into savings or use to go on vacation or something. I wanted to talk to someone about wanting to use some of that money to go on vacation, but not being able to because I had not yet conceived of a vacation that was good enough to use my Dead Parents Money on, but the person to talk to about this was not Vicente. The correct person to talk to might be a therapist, but I couldn't afford a therapist on my own, so then I would just be using Dead Parents Money to do that.

Vicente did not want to talk about dead people stuff. He wanted to talk about his kangaroo scrotum. It sounded like not just him, but his whole family was very attached to this cured ballsack of a dead animal. I wondered what it was like, to be so excited about inheriting something so stupid. For death and inheritance to be the novelty that it seemed to be, for him.

My phone buzzed again. I thought, Aww, somebody misses me.

"I'm gonna go see if that old guy's made any decisions," I said, handing the coin purse back to him. He stuck it back in the pocket of his chef jacket. The cooks didn't take the jackets home; they belonged to the restaurant and had to be left there, on a rack in the supply room. I wondered if Vicente ever arrived home to discover that he had forgotten to take the coin purse out of his pocket, and had to show up early the next day to locate it before the used jackets went to the cleaners.

The customer was still staring at the menu. He looked like he could use some help, but of course, he always gave off that vibe. It might just have been his face, the way everything turned downward at the corners. Mouth, eyebrows, even the crows' feet by his eyes seemed to sag helplessly. "Any questions I can answer for you?" I offered.

"No," he said. "I just need another minute. It's just . . . " Out came a tiny grunt, as if this were costing him some minor physical effort, like standing up from a crouch. I waited for him to finish the sentence, but he never did. It occurred to me that he probably did really want the salmon, but had already decided he was allergic, and so was stuck.

I was trapped between wanting to help him get unstuck, and wanting to get myself unstuck from the restaurant, although I was still at least an hour away from the possibility of leaving. Plus, leaving the restaurant would derail my own disappearing act. It would be a little too much self-advocacy for someone working on letting herself go. I had to find some third way that would make the restaurant situation less actively nerve-wracking without having to actually leave.

OBJECTS AT REST

In front of me, the customer muttered under his breath at the menu. Begging it to show him the way, or maybe cursing it. "You know," I told him, "one of our cooks has a coin purse made out of a kangaroo's scrotum."

The menu tilted down in his hands until it was resting flat on the table. "You don't say?"

"He's back there just whipping it around. Showing it to everyone." I did a check through my peripheral vision and couldn't see Chuck around anywhere. I bent down to whisper to the customer, "You didn't hear this from me, but he's not wearing gloves to touch the food. He's doing all this prep with his bare hands, and then he's also holding this scrotum."

The customer bit his lip. Of course, I had told him this in the hope that it would make *him* decide to leave so that I wouldn't have to, and my heart began to beat faster when I saw this. Not from excitement, understand, but because I was actively fighting the strange, protective instinct he inspired in order to do this. Pushing myself not to think about how fragile and helpless he would be outside of the restaurant, where decisions were unavoidable and time limited. If this man got behind the wheel of a car, he would certainly die. It was miraculous for him to have made it here in one piece to begin with.

And if he did die in a car crash on the way to his . . . house? Retirement condo? Hospital bed? then would he be leaving anyone behind, who would then have to live with his dead stuff? Who would worry about how to spend his dead money? I couldn't imagine what it would be like to lose someone to a car crash. I could only imagine major organ failure, which was what I had experience with. Mom's kidneys and Dad's heart.

"Do you think I could see it?" he said.

"Oh, believe me, I've seen it," I whispered.

"No, no, I believe you, I do. That's why I'm wondering if I could maybe get a look at it," said the customer. His jowls were practically vibrating. "It's been years since I've seen one."

"That's . . . " I stammered. "We're not really allowed to."

"You want to see Vicente's kangaroo purse?" said Chuck. He was standing right next to me. I started to scream, then turned it into a cough.

"Very much," said the customer.

"It's really something." Chuck smiled. "I'll talk to him. Anything else we can help you with?"

The customer looked at the menu, sitting on the table, without touching it. He sighed, shoulders slouching even more than they already had been. "Not yet. Oh! Could I get another diet coke?"

I switched back into service mode. "I'll get that right out for you!" I'd been waiting tables so long it was like I was under a spell. My phone buzzed impotently in my pocket. Can't talk now, I've been ensorceled. I imagined—fantastically—that my brother had been the one texting me all evening, having finally dedicated himself to forming a more genuine connection with his only living immediate relative. I felt a pang of cynical-hopeful-sadness as I thought this. Because, I knew, I was fantasizing about something I wanted, and if he had taken no real steps toward making it happen, then neither had I. Nobody at the restaurant even knew that I had a brother. Or that my parents were dead. It still wasn't too late to stop my brother from becoming a figment of my imagination the way they had, but he would if I let waitressing swallow me completely.

It occurred to me, for the first time, that I might not want to let myself go and disappear. But what did that even look like? Maybe, if I were more like my brother, then I would know how to stop letting the restaurant consume my life, but this just didn't seem like a real possibility. I didn't have more interesting things to zoom off to instead. I only had myself, and my collections of dead things.

When I came back with the diet coke, all three of them were clustered around the customer's chair. The customer, Chuck, and Vicente. The customer was holding the coin purse, gently rubbing it between his thumb and forefinger, nodding.

"It's really something," said Chuck, which I could have sworn I had heard him say a minute ago.

"You can't get them anymore," said Vicente. "They're illegal in Australia. That's where they come from."

I set the diet coke on the table, reaching across from the other side so as to stand as far away from them as possible.

"Oh, I know," said the customer. "It's been years since I've seen one."

"Are they really valuable?" Chuck asked.

OBJECTS AT REST

"Well . . . no," said the customer. "Beauty is in the eye of the beholder, though. That's what they say."

"It certainly is," said Chuck.

"It was my abuelo's," said Vicente. "He left it to me."

Thankfully, I had a couple more tables, some other late diners. I left the three of them, hunched over their little fetish.

From that point on, I resolved not to return to the customer's table unless he called me over, or if Chuck got on my case, but none of those things happened. Still, I couldn't stop looking over at him. I couldn't let go of the notion that he was in some kind of distress. After all the trouble he'd caused, he still begged to be attended to. The scrotum party eventually disbanded, and he went back to staring at the menu for a brief time, before turning his attention to his phone.

When my other tables had paid and gone, I looked at the clock and realized it was 9:50 p.m. That was when I had to return to the customer, who was still in the exact state I had last seen him.

"Hey!" I said cheerfully. "Just wanted to let you know, the kitchen is closing in ten minutes, so if you want to put in a food order, we'll need to get it in there pretty soon."

"Oh gosh." He fumbled his phone back into his pocket and picked the menu up. "Uh, just give me one more minute. Could I get another diet coke?"

After setting the refill on the table, I went straight to the bathroom and splashed water on my face, wet a paper towel, and started scrubbing self-destructively at my eyeliner. "You remember the first time you told me you needed *one more minute?*" I hissed at my reflection. "It was *two hours ago*. Do you even fucking know what a minute is, you chode?" This, I felt, would greatly upset the customer if I said it directly to him. So I said it to myself, in the mirror, two more times. Then I heard a toilet flush and Gabriella, the hostess, came out of the farthest stall.

"Hey," she said, washing her hands. "You good?"

"I'm good," I said. This was not true. I was mortified that someone had heard me grumbling at my reflection, and the worst of it was that I was not worried that I had upset Gabriella. I felt guilty in the customer's direction, as if Gabriella hearing what I said might upset him by some kind of psychic proxy.

"You good," she said, as a statement this time. "I'll wipe down tables and put up chairs, you vacuum?"

"Oh, uh, yeah," I said.

Chuck startled me again as I was vacuuming the floor around the bar, with most of the restaurant already done. I contented myself that the sound of the vacuum had drowned out my *Eeep!* when he said hey.

"I'd appreciate if you could avoid sweeping too near our guest." He always called vacuuming *sweeping* and it made me grind my teeth every time. He tilted his head in the direction of the customer, as if there were any other guests in the building.

"Okay," I said.

"We don't want him to feel like we're kicking him out," said Chuck.

"It's 10:30," I said. "We close at 10. Are we not kicking him out?"

"We've got it all covered," said Chuck. "We aren't turning off the grill or oven or fryer yet, so we should be able to make a plate real quick before we shut down. He just needs another minute." He dusted his hands together, perhaps to signify that he had been working hard, or perhaps to signify that he had been touching scrotum. "When stuff like this happens, you have to roll with the punches."

"Roll with the punches," I repeated.

"That's right," he said. "Honestly, I don't see why this should be so hard for you. I've been talking to him, he's a great guy, he just needs a little patience. Old people need patience sometimes. You've probably never dealt with an elderly relative, otherwise you'd know that. Just give him a minute. He'll get there."

I wanted to spit in his face but didn't. I also didn't want to open up to anyone at work about my family and exactly what I had dealt with, which I would have to if I stood up to Chuck now.

"Hey, you're doing fine," he said, dealing me an unwelcome, open-palm blow to the shoulder blades. "Just try not to make him feel uncomfortable."

By 11 o'clock, it was clear that the entire quarter of the restaurant surrounding the customer's table wasn't going to get cleaned, so I returned the vacuum to the supply room out back. There was a strong wind blowing that night, making it hard to open the supply room door or to keep my hair out of my face while opening it. Inside, I sat on a crate of paper towels and took my flats

OBJECTS AT REST

off. I wanted to massage my feet, but they felt angry enough to bite if touched, so I left them to their own devices to air out for a few minutes, confident I wasn't missing much inside the restaurant.

Sam, another one of the cooks, an older guy who worked pantry because his arthritic hands were still somehow amazing with knives, came in to hang up his chef jacket. "I've been cut," he explained. "If that guy wants a salad, someone else gonna have to make it. You think he wants a salad?"

"No." I thought back to his hand-wringing about wild caught salmon. "I think he might be allergic."

"To salad?"

I shrugged. He shrugged.

"Vicente." Sam's voice dropped an octave, and a few decibels. "He showed you the scrotum?"

"Uh, yeah?" It felt like one of the gotcha questions other kids would ask on the playground in grade school, to see if you knew what the word *scrotum* meant. I got the sense that, regardless of my answer, I was about to get giggled at. "So?" I added, hoping to cover my ass.

"He loves that thing," said Sam.

I looked at Sam. He looked at me. I no longer had any sense of where this was supposed to go. "Yes?" I said.

Sam gave another shrug, hung up his jacket on the dirty rack, and left.

Just as he turned outside of the supply room, Chuck's head and shoulders popped into view on one side of the doorframe, like a jump scare in a horror movie. I did jump. And scream. He showed no reaction. His hair didn't even react to the wind, him having none.

"Hey, what are you doing out here?" he said. "That guy's ready to order."

I hopped up and followed him back into the restaurant, shoes somehow already on my feet. "Why didn't you take his order?" I said as we maneuvered through the kitchen toward the dining room.

Chuck winced. "Well, he didn't actually ask to place an order. He just asked for you. But I assume that means he's ready."

I smoothed out the front of my apron as I approached the table. Honestly, I knew what was coming. I didn't even get my notepad out to take an order. I could see that the occupancy of the restaurant was down to just me, the customer, Chuck, and Vicente. Everybody outside his influence was gone, and with them, all pretense of us following any kind of social contract. It was in the air now, his miasma. He owned this place, and us.

"Oh!" said the customer. "There you are. Hey, I was wondering."

"Sure! What can I do for you?"

"Do you think you could talk to that cook again?"

I swallowed. "That cook."

"The one with the—"

"Talk to him?" I asked, though, of course, I knew what he meant. I tried to summon the defiance that had come over me in the bathroom mirror, but it wouldn't come. The miasma had me completely mired.

"Yeah." The customer had his palms flat on the table, as if bracing against it. Or, as if displaying them, so I could see that he wasn't doing some other, more insidious thing with them. "You know, about the—"

"I'll be right back."

I walked, as calmly as I could manage, back to the kitchen, then, almost at a run, out the back door and back to the supply room. I buried my face in as many of the dirty chef jackets as I could grab, my hands pressing them forcefully against the scream. Each time I inhaled to scream more I got hit with another tsunami of meat and cheese and balsamic vinegar smell. My face was absolutely going to break out from this if I didn't give it a good wash at home.

Why could I not do this to his face? What he was doing to us was so clearly, outrageously not okay. We simply could not resist. What was it about him?

I felt my phone buzz in my pocket. It seemed to be doing that unusually often. I didn't look at it, but I did think of my brother again. If I were more like my brother, I would not be in a situation like this. I would have left the restaurant hours ago, without looking back.

Why had the customer asked for me? Why not just ask Chuck to go get Vicente? He must have been somehow invested in my involvement, and why? What was he trying to do to me? Why did he insist on me being his caretaker?

OBJECTS AT REST

It was like he had targeted me because he could see into who I was in my heart. An object perpetually at rest. This was happening to me because I was the kind of person who would live, miserably, in the house of my dead parents, surrounded by their dead stuff, working my dead job, and occasionally going out to try to massage some life back into my dead friendships. He could sense this about me, somehow. That I could be tied down easily and not know how to escape. He knew this, and he was preying on me because of it. He was trying to keep me. And why? What did he want me for?

I returned to the kitchen, but Vicente wasn't there. *Oh thank god*, I thought, *he must have been cut too*. He's gone home to his . . . girlfriend? Dog? Playstation? Either way, I would have to tell the customer he couldn't see the gross coin purse. No way around it. Couldn't be done. The scrotum has left the building. He'd have to finally order or go home.

At first glance, his table looked vacant. I soon realized that he wasn't gone, he was sitting on the floor near the table, again with Chuck and Vicente. All of them sat cross-legged, in a little circle, like boys in a treehouse. Staring at something between them.

I cleared my throat, standing directly behind him. "Would you like to order anything?"

"Oh, uh, um." He fiddled with the waistband of his pants, which had sunk almost underneath him when he sat on the floor. He didn't manage to move it up much. "I'm," he said, "I'm fine. Uh, I'm good. Thank you."

"Okay," I chirped. The only sound for several seconds was the curiously strong wind outside. There wasn't much going on in the strip mall wasteland after 9 p.m. "Well, we don't want to hold you up if you need to get home."

"Actually, um." He looked theatrically around at the restaurant, nodding at empty tables, audibly breathing in when his gaze settled on the bar. "Actually, I like it here."

Looking over his shoulder, I could see that they had taken one of the napkins from the table and placed it, open, on the floor between them, like an altar cloth. The scrotum sat in the middle.

"You like it here," I repeated.

"You just go on home, tiger," said Chuck. He used *tiger* as if it were a familiar nickname, although he had never said it before. "We've got this. It's all under control. I'll see you at 4 tomorrow."

M.SHAW

"At 8," I corrected. "I'm working a double tomorrow."

"Right. At 8. Actually, you know what, go ahead and come in at 4. You're doing great. You've earned it."

The customer frowned. When he did this, it deepened a crease in his chin that created what almost looked like a second, fleshier frown. "Oh gosh, there's no reason why you should have to cut her hours," he said to Chuck. Was he talking about my shift the next day, or was he talking about me going home right now? My brain tried madly, vainly, to read the cues. "She may need the money. And she's doing such a good job."

Chuck tilted his head back, now frowning himself, appearing to stare through the ceiling. "She does do a great job," he muttered. "She's one of our best." He turned to me. "What do you think, tiger?"

Something inside me broke loose. I could almost hear it, like a guitar string snapping. "I think I could use the rest more," I said, barely managing not to choke on it. "My feet are really killing me."

I didn't stick around to argue further. I clocked out, threw my marinara-stained apron in the plastic grocery bag I kept in my purse, got in my car and drove the 12 miles back to my Dead Parents House. I was shaking like a frightened rabbit for the first 8 of those miles. Like I had escaped real violence.

It was Wednesday night. Not many people on the road. I mumbled to myself the whole way. What had the customer come to the restaurant expecting to get out of his evening? Had he been looking to stay there all along? Did he want to live in the restaurant, or what? Over and over, I shook my head, thinking of the three men on the floor, worshipping. I had the feeling that I had watched them disappear, before my eyes, the way I had been trying to myself for the past three months. I really had just escaped a kind of death.

I didn't check my phone until I got home, but I did feel it buzz twice more during the drive. All of the notifications were texts from my brother, saying variations of *please call me* with mounting urgency.

I'll keep this part short. My brother had stage four pancreatic cancer. So, if you're not familiar, pancreatic cancer, pretty much, if you get it, you're dead. It isn't detectable until so late in the game that, by the time you learn about it, it's almost always too late. And

OBJECTS AT REST

he had waited a long time to get checked out, figuring he was just sick. He wasn't going to do chemo. He told me all this over the phone, in the space of fifteen minutes. With Mom and Dad both gone within a year of each other, he was tired of coping. Tired of trying to live, tired of looking for reasons to, tired of fighting. I had never heard him talk like this before, never knew that he had any of these feelings about Mom and Dad, but I couldn't bring myself to say anything. It just made sense, he said. They were giving him a few months and he was using it to make peace.

I yelled at him, but only after we'd hung up. It was very important that, when I yelled at him, he not be able to hear me. I was the older sibling, and I wasn't used to showing that kind of vulnerability. And now, it was going to be too late to work on that. I didn't want to make peace; I wanted a relationship with my brother. I wanted us to fill the parent-less familial void for each other. I wanted to see him, one day, grow into the goofball uncle I knew he could be. Making peace is such a short thing, and I wanted length. Out of all the miserable shit I had let myself be tied to, he was the one person on Earth to whom I actually wanted that kind of attachment.

I screamed for most of the night, then called the restaurant and left a message that I wouldn't be coming in the next day, or for the foreseeable future. I explained that my brother was dying, and that my parents had just died as well, all of which was news to Ali, the Kitchen Manager who oversaw the a.m. shift. He didn't say much in response beyond "okay" and "good luck." I got the sense he was too intimidated by the sheer shittiness of it all, like he didn't want it to rub off on him by staying on the phone with me for too long.

I packed a suitcase and got the next available flight to Seattle. I was there for three months, taking care of my brother until he died. His Dead Parents Money, which he hadn't spent yet either, ended up being what paid for his funeral. I hung around the city for five more months, alone, staying on his friends' couches without ever really getting to know any of them. Then I got an English teaching job in Korea, and that's where I've been since. My parents' house sits, empty of everything except their dead people stuff, on the other side of the world. I almost never think about it.

Nobody understands what it is to be truly alone until they are. That's what I've decided. Unless they have been there too, it is impossible to communicate to anyone what it is like to know that you could disappear at any moment, and the only person who would notice is the one who would have to remove you from some company's payroll. I have become, at last, a figment of my own imagination. I and my brother were never opposites; we were both self-destructing, only in different ways. The difference between us is that I found a way out of my self-destruction, and his killed him. If I had managed to figure my shit out sooner, could I have been there to tell him to go to the doctor when the pain started? I wonder about this all the time, and I do it knowing that even this is a grasping to reclaim something already gone. That I am already gone.

I never went back to the restaurant, and for all I know, the three of them are still sitting there, clustered around that thing. *You can't get them anymore. It's really something. Roll with the punches. It's been years since I've seen one. Sometimes these things just happen. It was my abuelo's. Could I get another diet coke?*

And look: my last night in that place, it was weird. It doesn't make sense and I don't understand most of what went on. It hasn't been relevant to my life in any continuing way, and I've never had the bandwidth to really process any of it in the time since. Except one thing. Except this:

Towards the end, when my brother was barely able to recognize that I was even in the room, when his body was actively failing around him, when he couldn't annunciate his words, when he'd usually already shit himself by the time he realized he had to go, he looked like the customer. The slope of the eyebrows. The chin. The constantly slightly open mouth. The thousand-yard stare. He looked just like him. The vulnerability and helplessness. The way his very presence compelled you to attend to him. In the grip of something that wouldn't let him go until the end. Afflicted. Nothing left for him but suffering unto death.

In that moment, I saw that he and I had switched places. Now he was the one at rest, the one tied down. To his illness, specifically, which would soon put him at rest for good. I, for all my inability to move on from things, was the one still in motion. I wondered if the way he looked to me now was the way I had looked to him, in earlier years. Maybe to others, as well.

OBJECTS AT REST

I think the customer recognized in me a kindred spirit. And I think I understand that what he really wanted me for was a friend. He was just going about that through the only way of interacting with the world he knew: through inertia. Maybe he found what he was looking for a little more successfully with Chuck, or even Vicente, but it was clear that he had really wanted me. I was the most inert of all of them, and he saw that, and that made me see it too. The only thing I don't know is how I finally managed to shake myself loose, at that pivotal moment. Maybe there was a little bit of my brother in me, after all.

Sometimes I imagine my brother, as he looked before he died, taking his last breath and then, at the end of all the pain, finding himself walking into a restaurant. Not a fine establishment, a Golden Restaurant in the Sky or anything like that. A casual place with booths and a bar and "Grille" in the name, poorly lit, where they give you bread and free refills. Comfortable. Safe. He sits down and, right there, he has all the control he could ever want of his environment, with no responsibility to anyone. A place where the biggest decision he'll ever need to make is what to order, and it's not a binding decision. They're always open and never slow, but also never crowded. His smartphone never runs out of battery, and the signal is always great.

A place he never needs to leave. I'm not sure if it's Heaven or Hell.

ACKNOWLEDGMENTS

A fact that everyone who reads this ought to be aware of is that Matt Blairstone and Alex Woodroe of Tenebrous Press are very clearly not of this world. Every conversation I have within the writing community about the publisher of this book involves some variant of us wondering, *who the hell are these people? How are they doing this? Why is everything they release so good?*

I do not have the answers to any of these questions, but I have sure as hell been the beneficiary of them, in the form of both my previous book and this one. In the case of *All Your Friends Are Here*, the book was Alex and Matt's idea before it was mine; in the process of acquiring its predecessor, *One Hand to Hold, One Hand to Carve*, they suggested that I should send them a short story collection next. A year or so later, I sent them a panoply of *Fraught With Ennui*™ stories along a general theme, which they refined into the book you're holding. The fact that you're holding it is down to their work as much as mine.

In fact, there's a whole category of people without whom this book might very well have never arrived. I spent most of 2022 and 2023 centrally enmeshed in a *very* nasty fight over union contract bargaining with Meow Wolf Denver LLC, which wrecked my mental health and nearly put me in the hospital. Suffice to say, I was not doing much writing during this time, and I owe my profound thanks to the people in my life who pulled me out of it. Most especially Renita, Anya, Jesse, Nikki, Matt, Cooper, and my parents. Without them, I believe the most I would have been able to offer the world would have been a single cautionary tale, rather than a whole story collection.

Maybe this is corny, but I do want to shoutout the readers as well, especially the ones who flip to the acknowledgments page to figure out who is to blame. If that's the info you're looking for, then let me be clear: it's you. We do this without support from big capital, from major publishing houses, or even an agent, in my case. These books keep happening because of you. There's no one to blame but yourself. Keep it up; you're part of an amazing time in literary history.

ABOUT THE CONTRIBUTORS

M. Shaw (they/them) is generally understood to be a masked brigand who robs from the rich and gives to the poor in the Colorado front range. Their novella *One Hand to Hold, One Hand to Carve* received the 2022 Wonderland Book Award for novel/novella of the year. Their website is mshawesome.com and they stay away from social media because it really is just dreadfully unpleasant.

Echo Echo is a Portuguese artist and a proponent of *horror vacui*. She immerses herself in individual pieces for up to a year at a time and renders in extreme detail. Echo also performs in multiple bands, finding equal freedom in expressing herself through music as she does through illustration.

Some stories have been previously published. They originally appeared in:

Apex Magazine (The Cure for Loneliness)
Cast of Wonders (As I Wait for the Killing Blow)
Cosmic Contact: First Contact Stories (One Long Staircase, Just Going Up)
Cosmic Horror Monthly (Roots in the Ground)
Crossed Genres (The Only Friend You Ever Need)
The Dread Machine (Apartémon)
Fantasy Magazine (Man vs. Bomb)
Fireside Fiction (As I Wait for the Killing Blow)
SF Magazine (The Cure for Loneliness)
Valparaiso Fiction Review (Objects at Rest)
Voyage YA (My Dad Bought a Space Shuttle)
We're Here: the Best Queer Speculative Fiction 2022 (My Dad Bought a Space Shuttle)

The following stories have been edited since their original publication: Man vs. Bomb; One Long Staircase, Just Going Up; As I Wait for the Killing Blow; The Cure for Loneliness; The Only Friend You Ever Need.

CONTENT WARNINGS

Being a work of mature Horror, a degree of violence, gore, sex and/or death is to be expected. For more specific concerns, please check the alphabetized list below for specific potential triggers suggested by the author.

Ableist Language: The Motorist

Alcohol Use: Go with the Flow, My Dad Bought a Space Shuttle, One Long Staircase, Ready Player (n+1), Roots in the Ground

Bad, Awkward, and/or Painful Sex: Go with the Flow, The Only Friend You Ever Need, Roots in the Ground

Cannibalism: Apartémon, Man vs. Bomb

Child Abuse: My Dad Bought a Space Shuttle

Christianity References: The Only Friend You Ever Need, Ready Player (n+1)

Climate Change References: The Apology, One Long Staircase

Death of a Parent: As I Wait for the Killing Blow, Objects at Rest, Roots in the Ground

Death of a Pet: The Cure for Loneliness, The Motorist

Dendrophilia: Roots in the Ground

Dismemberment: As I Wait for the Killing Blow, Go with the Flow

Drug Use: The Cure for Loneliness, My Dad Bought a Space Shuttle, Ready Player (n+1)

Family Estrangement: The Motorist, My Dad Bought a Space Shuttle, Objects at Rest, Ready Player (n+1), Roots in the Ground

Genital Mutilation: The Apology, Objects at Rest, Roots in the Ground

Gore: Go with the Flow, Man vs. Bomb, The Motorist, The Only Friend You Ever Need

Home Invasion: The Only Friend You Ever Need

Imprisonment: Apartémon, Man vs. Bomb, Ready Player (n+1)

Loss of Bodily Autonomy: Ready Player (n+1)

Mutilation of a Corpse: The Only Friend You Ever Need

Police Presence: The Motorist

Revenge Porn References: The Motorist

Scatological References: The Motorist, My Dad Bought a Space Shuttle, Ready Player (n+1)

Stalking: The Cure for Loneliness, The Motorist

Toxic Masculinity: The Apology, The Cure for Loneliness, The Motorist, My Dad Bought a Space Shuttle, One Long Staircase, Ready Player (n+1), Roots in the Ground

Transphobia: The Motorist, My Dad Bought a Space Shuttle, Ready Player (n+1)

Violence Toward Non-Human Animals: Apartémon, Man vs. Bomb, Objects at Rest, Ready Player (n+1)

Grab another Tenebrous title!

Grab another Tenebrous title!

TENEBROUS PRESS

aims to drag speculative fiction into newer, Weirder territory with stories that are incisive, provocative and intelligent; delivered by voices diverse and unsung.

FIND OUT MORE:
www.tenebrouspress.com

@TenebrousPress on social media

HAIL NEW WEIRD LIT.

HAIL THE TENEBROUS CULT.